PRAISE FOR JACK QUAID

Escape from Happydale is part *Buffy*, part *Halloween*, with a touch of wry humor in between. A bloody good tale!

LAURA B., PROOFREADER, RED ADEPT
PUBLISHING

This book should come with a warning and that warning should read: DON'T MAKE ANY DAMN PLANS!

SPACE AND THUNDER MAGAZINE

Give JACK QUAID a typewriter, a bottle of bourbon and two weeks and he'll give you a novel that blows your socks off!

DANIEL S PERRY, AUTHOR OF THE
'MECHA MAN' SERIES

ESCAPE FROM HAPPYDALE

THE LAST FINAL GIRL

JACK QUAID

ELECTRIC MAYHEM

WHAT THE HELL IS THIS NOVEL ABOUT?

Stephen King meets Quentin Tarantino

At the end of every horror movie, one girl always survives the deadly slasher… In this case, Parker Ames not only survives, she turns the tables and dedicates her life to hunting and destroying the monsters that stalk slumber parties and campsites all across the country.

Ten years after the horrific events known as the Massacre at Coffin Bay, Parker's world has been flipped totally upside down. She's no longer the nerdy teenage girl who would run and hide from the things that go bump in the night. Now Parker *is* the thing that goes bump in the night.

After years of traveling the country and hunting some of the world's most dangerous slashers, Parker returns home when she hears that Hurricane Williams, the deranged slasher who slaughtered her family, has resurfaced and continued his killing spree. Armed with her trusty chain saw, affectionately named Aerosmith, she sets out on a path of revenge and redemption.

WHO THE HELL IS JACK QUAID?

Between the years 1980 and 1999, American novelist Jack Quaid produced a series of fun and wild stories where anything could happen, and with Quaid behind the typewriter, they usually did. He called these books his Electric Mayhem series.

Jack Quaid was born in West Hollywood, California, in 1953. He won a scholarship to UCLA but dropped out after six months for a reason that, to this day, remains unknown. Two years later, he sold his first short story to Startling Mystery Magazine, but it was the publication of his novel The City on the Edge of Tomorrow in 1980 and the film adaptation starring Bruce Dern that set him on his way.

Fearing his initial success would fade, Quaid wrote obsessively for the next two decades and published under many pseudonyms. It's unknown just how many books he produced during this period, but despite the name on the jacket, savvy readers always knew they were reading a Jack Quaid novel within the first few pages.

His books have long been out of print, and they now live on the dusty shelves of secondhand bookstores and in the memories of those who have been lucky enough to read them.

Quaid's current whereabouts are unknown.

www.jackquaidbooks.com

INTRODUCTION

The book you hold in your hand has had a strange and unusual path to publication. It's a story which involved failed movie deals, gunfire, and *Ferris Bueller's Day Off's* very own Mia Sara, who played Sloan. But to tell the story of how this novel happened to be discovered, we need to go back to the '90s—1995, to be exact.

Now, back then, I was fifteen years old, and I'd never heard of Jack Quaid, *Escape from Happydale*, or any of the other unknown number of novels Quaid happened to punch out of his typewriter between the year 1980 and the year 1999. I didn't discover Jack Quaid until he was all but forgotten and his books were long out of print, but I can still remember that very first moment I held one of those books in my hand and all the promise the pages held within.

It was a Saturday afternoon, and I had nine dollars in my pocket and an entire afternoon to kill. At that age, any money I had was spent on either ex-rental videos or secondhand books. The VCR was broken, so I caught the train into Chicago with one destination in mind: Galaxy Books on Wabash. The secondhand bookstore specialized in two types of novels and two types of novels only—science fiction and horror. If you wanted romance, crime, or heaven forbid, literature, you were shown the door and ridiculed later by the proprietor, Gary G, whom I never saw wear anything other than his Camp Crystal Lake T-shirt.

The shelves were always overcrowded, and books were even stacked on the floor, reaching all the way to the ceiling. At first glance, the place looked like a panic attack, but to me, those thousands of dusty books were gateways to fantastical worlds, distant planets, and alternate dimensions where all kinds of crazy stuff could happen. It was from those stacks that I pulled my first Jack Quaid novel, *World War Metal*, from the bottom of a tower of books that was dangerously close to toppling over.

The paperback looked as if it had been read a thousand times by people who were in a hurry and on the move. The cover was creased and worn white at the edges, and the spine was cracked in a couple dozen places. At some point in the book's life, some-body had let a cigarette burn down in their fingers while reading, and it had singed a bunch of pages. Despite the wear and tear on that copy of the book, it didn't detract from the absolute madness of the faded art on the cover, though. Among the mayhem of robots and battle spiders was the heroine of the story, Abigail Storm, firing two blasters while jumping backward out of a burning building. I didn't even read the blurb; I just handed over my three dollars and walked out with my very first Jack Quaid novel. Up until that point, *World War Metal* was the most insane novel I had ever read. It was set in a 1980s vision of the future where the world's robots rise up to destroy humanity and the only thing standing in their way is a supermodel hell-bent on stopping them. It was John Carpenter, '80s neon pop, and Cyndi Lauper all rolled into one.

I read it in one night, and from that point on, I was hooked. For years, every single time I walked into a secondhand bookstore, I made a line for the Q section with hope that maybe, just maybe, I would discover another Jack Quaid novel. Most of the time, I left empty-handed, but every once in a while, in the dusty basements of bookshops and at secondhand fairs, I would find a new title. Over the years since I discovered *World War Metal*, I've found *The City on the Edge of Tomorrow*, *Star Blaster*, *San Angeles*, and a handful more. The worn and beaten paperbacks of Jack Quaid were the realms of mad bastards of literature where all bets were off, and if there were any rules to break, his books went out of their way to break them.

Fast forward fifteen years and three thousand miles, and I'm sitting in the office of schlock horror movie producer Marty Marshall. Three days earlier, Marty was at a party and mentioned that he had an idea for a horror movie and needed a writer. Somebody gave him my number, and there I was, sitting in his office above a tattoo parlor on Sunset Boulevard. The joint was a mess, with stacks of yellow-paged screenplays against the wall and the posters for *Chopping Mall, Girls Nite Out*, and *The Day After Halloween* on the walls. Each and every one of them was a hack 'n' slash classic.

Marty sat behind a big oak desk that was too big for the room. He had an oxygen tank by his side and a cigarette between his lips. "Listen up," he barked. "You're gonna love this title." He paused for a dramatic buildup. "*The Return of the Killer Kangaroos from Outta Space*." He slapped his hands together, smiled, and killed his cigarette in the ashtray. "What do yer think?"

I didn't think much. "Do you have any money for a script?"

"Money!" Marty snapped. "Hell no! You write the script, we make the movie, and everybody gets paid."

As if I needed another reason to get the hell out of there, just in that very moment, I heard gunfire, and a round blasted through the floor from the tattoo parlor below.

I nearly had a heart attack. "What the hell was that?"

Marty hadn't even flinched. "Oh, that," he said. "The guys downstairs get a little excited when they watch soccer and shoot their guns off."

There were a dozen or so bullet holes in the ceiling right above my head. "I think I'm probably going to go now, Marty."

"It's nothing to worry about. Trust me."

"No, Marty," I said climbing to my feet. "I think it is something to worry about."

"What about the movie?"

"I'll get back to you," I said, making my way to the door and trying to get the hell out of there as soon as I possibly could.

I was halfway between the massive oak desk and my escape when one of the manuscripts piled against the wall of Marty's office grabbed my attention. The cover page was old and yellow. At some point, somebody had spilt coffee or whiskey on it, but despite the mess, I could still make out the lettering on the cover.

ESCAPE FROM HAPPYDALE
by Jack Quaid

In all my years of combing secondhand bookstores, I had never seen or heard of anything called *Escape from Happydale*. I picked up the three-hundred-page manuscript, brushed the dust off the first page, and held it up to Marty. "What's this?"

The vintage producer picked up a pair of thick '70s-style glasses from his desk and pushed them up the bridge of his nose. It took a moment for his eyes to focus and read the cover, but when they did, he wasn't impressed with what he saw. "That son of a bitch, Jack Quaid."

"Where did you get it?"

"I hired that son of a bitch, Quaid, sometime back in the '80s to write me a horror movie for Mia Sara."

"*Ferris Bueller's Day Off* Mia Sara?"

"She was going to be a big star."

"But she wasn't."

"Which is why the movie was never made."

I thumbed through the first few pages. "This isn't a screenplay. It's a novel?"

"Tell me about it," Marty said as his nicotine-stained fingers reached for another cigarette and lit it. "He was one of those overachieving types. I gave that son of a bitch twenty K for a screenplay, and he delivered three novels and a goddamned screenplay. He told me that they were a trilogy. Back then, nobody knew what the hell a trilogy was. Nowadays, it's trilogy this and trilogy that."

"Do you have the other two novels?" I asked.

"Ah," Marty said with a swipe of his hand. "Who knows?"

"Can I read this?"

"Keep the damn thing," Marty said. "And if you see that son of a bitch, tell him he's a son of a bitch from me."

"What did he do?"

"He ran off with my wife and stole my Cadillac. I didn't care too much about the wife, but that Caddy, that was a good vehicle."

Two more rounds blasted through the floor of Marty Marshall's office, and I got the hell out of there. A couple of blocks later, I walked into the first dive bar I found, ordered a drink, and turned over the first page of the battered manuscript.

For the rest of the day and half the night, I was fifteen years old again and grinning ear to ear as I read every single last word. That manuscript, dear reader, is the novel you now hold in your hands.

Escape from Happydale is Jack Quaid at his most rebellious, at his most sincere, and certainly at his most unpredictable. For those of you who have read Jack Quaid over the years, welcome back. You've been here before, and you know what you're getting into. But for those of you who are experiencing a Jack Quaid tale for the first time, I have a word of advice. Draw the shades, pour yourself a tall drink, turn some rock 'n' roll up loud, and strap in.

See you on the other side.

Luke Preston
Barkowski, Santa Monica

ESCAPE FROM HAPPYDALE

Only one of you will survive.

OLD HORROR PROVERB

1988

ONE

NANCY SINCLAIR WAS in the middle of nowhere when the fuel light on the dashboard lit up. She peered through the dirty windshield then into the rearview mirror and saw darkness in both directions.

"This is totally going to suck," she mumbled to herself.

The year was 1988, and if there ever had been a time when it was safe for a nineteen-year-old girl to be stranded in the middle of the night, in the middle of nowhere, that time had certainly passed. She was somewhere between Cedar Springs and Happydale on an old dirt road that officially didn't have a name. Unofficially, the kids called it Resurrection Road. The story went that back in the '60s, a series of young girls had disappeared while traveling along the old road and were never seen or heard from again. Some believed they were abducted and murdered by a crazed lunatic who roamed the rural outskirts of Happydale. Others believed the girls were sacrificed by a satanic cult. A few even believed the disappearing girls were the work of a *Texas Chain Saw Massacre*–style family who lived off the grid, killing hitchhikers and tourists whenever they had the opportunity. Nancy always thought the stories were rubbish. That was until she found herself on Resurrection Road with no fuel and no idea how far away the next gas station was. But she always believed one thing—no matter how mad or crazy a story was, deep down, there was always a hint of truth in it.

Nancy nervously tapped her thumb on the steering wheel, kept her eyes glued to the dark road ahead, and prayed for a miracle. Then out of the darkness, like a desert oasis, that miracle came. She leaned forward, peered through the windshield, and saw the flashing neon lights of Patrick's Garage & Gas emerge from the darkness.

Relief washed over her as she pulled her mother's 1979 Chevy Nova into the filling station and shut the engine down by the single fuel pump. She glanced out the window at the empty worn-down, beat-down service station and saw nothing but empty shelves through the dirty windows and no sign of life whatsoever anywhere inside.

Nancy was two seconds away from declaring the joint abandoned. She was about to turn the engine back over and hit the road when she saw a dark figure off to the side of the gas station.

He held something in his hands. Nancy couldn't really make out what it was. She leaned forward to get a closer look. The figure swung the object high up above his head where the moonlight caught it before it slammed back down hard and fast.

It was an ax.

"Oh, to hell with this," Nancy said to herself as she turned the key to crank the engine, but the son of a bitch wouldn't start. It just chugged and chugged, and all that chugging drew the attention of the dark figure with the ax, and ax in hand, he started to make his way over.

Nancy pumped the gas. She yelled, and she cursed, but nothing was starting that Chevy Nova. The dark figure moved closer, and with his every step, she saw more of him. He was a big bastard, must have been close to six and a half feet tall, with massive hands and skin like leather. Then as he neared the car and stepped into the light, Nancy could see that maybe he wasn't really all that menacing at all. Despite being huge and slightly creepy looking, he could easily have passed for any other regular guy… maybe.

His overalls were covered in grease and ketchup, but Nancy could still make out the name patch on his shirt, just over his heart. It was Patrick, and Patrick's Garage & Gas was apparently his place.

He rapped a big knuckle on the glass. "You after a fill-up, girly?"

She stared at him for a moment, weighed up her options and realized she didn't have any. "I need gas."

"We'll have you back on the road soon enough," Patrick said.

He leaned the ax up against the pump, pulled the hose, and began filling the Chevy Nova with gas while he whistled away.

The entire time Patrick was back there, Nancy couldn't take her eyes off the ax. It was old, and that old ax had seen plenty of action over the years. The handle was well worn with notches and scratches, but the blade wasn't rusty or tarnished. It was silver and sharp, and it looked as if it could hack clean through a log—or Nancy—with just one blow.

Was she overreacting? Was she not overreacting enough? Was she going to be chopped up into a thousand little pieces and end up a cautionary horror tale told at slumber parties? The horror movie of her own demise ran through her mind in fast-forward, and the entire time, she still couldn't take her eyes off the ax.

When Patrick knocked on the glass with his massive hands, he broke her concentration, and she almost jumped out of her skin. "Eight dollars. Thanks, girly."

Nancy shuffled around in her handbag for a moment, found her wallet, and pulled out her MasterCard. She wound down the window a tiny little, itsy-bitsy crack, just enough to slip the card through to Patrick.

"You're going to have to come inside if you want to use that card, miss." He thumbed back at the filling station. "The machine's in there. Stuck to the bench, you see."

She shifted her gaze beyond Patrick to the isolated gas station and back to him. "I don't have any cash."

"Then I think it's looking like you might have to come inside. I don't bite." He grinned, exposing a couple of missing teeth.

After some internal deliberation, Nancy unlocked the door, climbed out, and followed Patrick across the grease-stained concrete and into Patrick's Garage & Gas. She took a couple of tentative steps as she saw the empty shelves and dirty floors. She was starting to think she had made a terrible decision.

"Now, sweetheart. I'm about to do something, and I don't want you to go and get your panties all in a knot about it, all right?" Patrick said as he made his way around the counter.

Fear washed over her. That feeling of making a terrible decision was no longer just a feeling. In Nancy's mind, it was a full-blown fact.

She took half a step back. "What are you going to do?"

Patrick flicked a switch behind the counter, and Nancy heard the door lock, the very same door she had just walked though and would need to escape through if all went to hell.

"Oh, shit!" Nancy wrapped her fingers around the handle and violently shook the doors, but no matter how much shaking she did, it was pretty clear, she wasn't getting out in a hurry. She turned back to Patrick. "What the fuck, Patrick!"

"Calm down, girly. Take a deep breath and calm down."

"Open this door, you psycho!"

"Now," Patrick said. "I don't think that would be the best idea going around town right now."

She threw up her fists. "I'm a black belt." And although she was trying to look menacing, it was as clear as day that she hadn't thrown a punch in her life.

Patrick held up his hands. "In the back seat of your car, there's a man, and this man, he's holding a great big bastard of a knife."

Slowly, Nancy lowered her fists and looked out the window, across the concrete, and over at her mother's Chevy Nova. From the inside of Patrick's Garage & Gas, the back seat of her car appeared empty, but it was too far and too dark for her to really tell for sure.

"I needed to get you out of the car without alarming him."

She looked back at Patrick. "Bullshit."

"No," he said. "That's not bullshit."

"Unlock this door," she said.

"No way, José."

Nancy wasn't taking no for an answer. She scanned the service station products, spotted a shovel for five dollars, gripped it in her hands it, and held that shovel up, ready to swing. "You've got to the count of three, and then you're going to open this door."

Patrick was defiant. "I don't think so, girly."

"One," she said.

"There's something out there."

"Two," she said.

"Something bad."

"Three." And with all her strength, she swung the

shovel back, and just as she was about to smash it clear through the glass door of Patrick's Garage & Gas, Nancy stopped dead.

On the other side of the window was Hurricane Williams. That scary son of a bitch was standing there in a filthy orange prison jumpsuit with a monster of a machete in his hand that looked big enough to chop down a tree. And over his head was a hood, the kind they put on prisoners just before they're about to be read their last rites and executed.

Nancy screamed. She dropped the shovel, and when she looked back, Hurricane had disappeared. "What the fuck was that!" she yelled.

Patrick pointed an old tobacco-stained finger at her. "I told you. I goddamned told you!"

She shook the door. "Are you sure this thing is locked?"

"My word it is." Then his face dropped as if he'd just remembered something life-changing.

"What is it?" Nancy asked.

"Back door!" Patrick turned on his heels and took off running across the gas station. He busted through a back door and continued down the hall, with Nancy not far behind.

The back door was one of those doors with a small glass window in the middle, and before Patrick was even there, the hooded face appeared in the dirty window.

"Hurry!" Nancy yelled.

The handle turned. The door opened an inch just before Patrick slid hard and fast into it, slamming that door shut again. With his weight pushed up against it, there was no way known Hurricane was going to push through. Patrick dug his fingers into his pocket, pulled out his keys, and dropped them.

"Pick them up!" Nancy yelled. "Pick them up!"

Patrick scooped them into his hands and slid the key into the lock. A flick of the wrist later, the door was shut and locked. Hurricane looked at him for a brief moment through the dirty window then disappeared as if he had never been there at all.

Nancy's heart finally started to slow a beat.

Patrick caught his breath, leaned against the door, and looked back at Nancy with a satisfied smile. "Don't worry, girly. He's gone."

Patrick had spoken too soon—way too soon.

A great big machete slammed through the door, and straight after that, it slammed through Patrick's back then out of his chest. A bead of blood dripped off the tip of the blade and onto the cheap vinyl floor.

"Oh my," Nancy said. "That's not good."

Hurricane yanked the blade out, and Patrick's

body slumped to the floor like nothing more than the hunk of dead meat that it was.

"That's really not good." She stumbled back a couple of steps into the store. Except for the hum of the neon lights outside, everything was deathly quiet. Nancy took slow, careful, and quiet steps as she moved through the store with her eyes peeled on the windows, just looking and waiting for anything that moved.

There was a phone on the wall, and Nancy's slow and considered steps took her toward it. She wedged the receiver between her ear and neck and dialed 911.

It rang… and rang… and rang… then a voice answered. "Happydale Police."

"There's some nutcase at Patrick's Garage & Gas. He's trying to kill me. You gotta come."

"Is Patrick there?"

"He's dead. Patrick's dead."

There was a pause followed by a scared voice. "How?"

"Stabbed! Are you on your way or…"

Click. The line went dead.

"Oh, for fuck's sake." She hung up the phone and was about to step away from the counter when she saw Patrick's ax lying on it. "Looks like it's you and me," she said as she scooped up the tool.

She tried out a couple of swinging attack moves,

but it was heavy, and Nancy didn't really know what she was doing. So each practice swing looked as if it would do more damage to herself than anyone she was trying to inflict damage on. Considering the situation, she figured the ax was all she had. So she gripped it in her hands and made her way through the building.

Nancy scanned the yard, the gas pumps, and the darkness that surrounded them. Everything was quiet and calm. Under any other circumstances, one could even say it was peaceful. She settled her gaze on the Chevy Nova, which given the circumstances, was her only way out of this hell.

Nancy found the switch behind the desk, and when she flicked it, the lock on the door disengaged. The entrance door opened a crack. Trying not to make a sound, she pulled open the door, stepped through, and closed the door gently behind her. The walk to the Chevy Nova was short, but with the scared baby steps she was taking, it might as well have been one hundred miles away.

Hurricane was out there. She knew that much. She just didn't know where or when the big bastard would strike.

She tightened her grip on the ax and kept her eyes peeled. The closer she got to the car, the more her confidence grew and the quicker her steps became.

When she finally reached that Chevy Nova, Nancy pulled open the door and climbed inside. Giddy with relief over almost having a clean getaway, she turned the key, and the engine roared to life on the first try. She grinned from ear to ear. Nancy had heard those stories about Resurrection Road, and she was going to be the one who made it out. She was going to be the one to live and tell the tale. No one was going to tell the tale of her death at a slumber party.

That's what she thought, anyway… until she flicked on the headlights.

Hurricane Williams was standing right there at the front of the Chevy Nova. He raised the machete high and slammed it down hard and fast, straight through the hood and into the engine.

The motor shuddered, spat, and sputtered, and a moment later, it was dead.

The maniac had just murdered the car.

Nancy let out a god-awful scream, then just as quickly as he'd appeared, Hurricane was gone again.

When her scream died, Nancy tried to get a grip on herself. She cocked her head and looked out the windows.

Where the hell is he?

Who cares? she thought after a moment. There was no point sticking around to find out. She turned the key, pumped the gas, turned the key, and pumped the gas again. It was time to get the hell out of there, but no matter how hard she tried, the car was as dead as disco.

"Damn it," she snapped, and then she saw something out of the corner of her eye. It was the button to her door; it was up! She slammed it down with the palm of her hand and then worked her way around the car, locking the other three doors, and once she'd done that, Nancy slammed back into her seat and sigh with relief, thinking she was safe.

Which was of course, she was not.

Nancy heard a sound on the roof, but at best, she had only a fraction of a second to react, and a fraction of a second wasn't much time to do much of anything. A great big machete slammed through the roof of the car and missed Nancy's face by inches.

She threw herself across to the passenger seat and ducked down low.

The blade slammed through the roof again.

And again…

And again…

And again…

All the while, Nancy darted around the small, enclosed stab trap, dodging blows she didn't even know were coming. It was just a matter of time before she was hit. There was one thought and one thought only running through Nancy's mind: *Get the hell out of here.*

Nancy popped up the button, kicked the door open, and rolled out of the car onto the grease-stained concrete. She rolled onto her back and scurried backward toward the filling station, but nobody ever got far in that position, so when Hurricane jumped off the roof of the car, he landed right at Nancy's feet.

Toying with her, stalking her, Hurricane lurked over Nancy as she crawled backward until she reached the gas station, and when she'd made it that far, there was nowhere else to go. Nancy was trapped. It was the end of the line, and she knew it. She was beat and drenched in fear, and when she spoke, her voice shuddered.

"Please," she said. "Please."

Hurricane paused, as if he were giving the idea of letting her go real due consideration. But that was never going to happen. He raised the blade. A glint of moonlight bounced off it, and just as he was ready to slam it down and end Nancy's life, a voice called out from behind him.

"Hey, dickhead."

Hurricane slowly looked over his shoulder. The girl behind him couldn't have been more than twenty-five years old, but in those twenty-five years, she had lived a lifetime. Even from a distance, Nancy could make out the scuffed Doc Martens on her feet, the blue jeans, her *Save Ferris* tee, her leather racing jacket, and long blond hair, which she wore down. From a distance, she was just another all-American girl. Up close was an entirely different story. She had scars on her knuckles from a hundred fistfights and a faint scar across her throat from when one of those fights almost hadn't gone her way. In one hand, she had a .45, and in the other was a machete. One thing was for sure: she hadn't come to play nice.

Her name was Parker Ames.

"It's my guess that you wear that mask for a reason," Parker said. "And I'm guessing that reason probably isn't a pretty one."

Hurricane looked from Parker to Nancy and back to Parker again as if trying to decide who to kill first. And then he stepped toward Parker, his choice made.

A smirk grew into the corner of her mouth as she glanced down at the machete in his hand. "Really?"

She raised the .45, wrapped her finger around the trigger, and squeezed.

Bang!

Bang!

She put two in his chest, and he dropped to the ground. Everything fell quiet.

Even lying down, he was a massive bastard, and

when Parker stepped forward, she did so very, very carefully. She holstered the .45 on her hip and wrapped both hands around her machete handle.

Nancy leaned forward. "Is… is he dead?"

Just then, Hurricane roared to life and sat up with his own blade in his hand.

Parker didn't miss a beat. She raised her machete over her head and slammed it down nice and hard through his chest.

Once wasn't enough for Parker, though. She pulled the machete out, rammed it back into his chest, and hit repeat on that move over and over again. Blood sprayed everywhere. On Parker, on Nancy, and all over the concrete at Patrick's Garage & Gas.

Nancy watched that massacre for what felt like forever, and there was only one word to describe it. And that word was *overkill*.

Parker raised the machete high in the sky. She was going in for the death blow, intending to lob the evil son of a bitch's head clean off. Then at the last moment… she paused.

Flashing red and blue lights flooded the scene, and when Parker looked over her shoulder, a young Happydale deputy was hanging out of his patrol car with his gun aimed squarely at her.

He looked at the girl covered in blood, the

machete in her hand, and the body at her feet. The deputy had only one question on his mind: *What the fuck is going on here?*

"I promise you," Parker said, "this really isn't what it looks like."

TWELVE HOURS EARLIER

TWO

THE PARIS, Texas, mental asylum was the mental asylum where patients were sent when they were kicked out of all the other mental asylums. Nate Jackson had grown up in the area and heard all the rumors, but it wasn't until he got a part-time job as a nurse-slash-guard that he realized the stories didn't even scratch the surface of the reality.

It was Nate's second day, and he was already strapping on the riot gear. It wasn't exactly a good sign of things to come. *To hell with it,* he thought. He was only doing the job until he saved enough money to move to LA and start a band. He just had to tough it out for the next few months, and then Paris, Texas, would be nothing but a bad dream.

"Use the tape, not the Velcro," Beans said as he pointed to a roll on the bench in the changing room.

"These nuts have got mad strength. They'll tear all that armor right off your body."

Nate had been assigned to Beans and was told to shadow him to learn the ropes. In the morning, Beans had taken him for a tour of the asylum. In the afternoon, he'd introduced Nate to all the residents, and by early evening, he watched as Beans beat the hell out of some poor bastard just to, in Beans's own words, "keep them straight."

"You've got to keep them straight," he would say. Nate didn't know why Beans thought they needed to be kept straight, and he figured the patients didn't either. He was a big guy who had probably worked out or played football in his teenage years, but that was a long time ago, and any muscle he may have had had been eroded by bottles of Budweiser and buckets of fried chicken. Beer and chicken aside, Beans was a big bastard who knew how to handle himself, so when he told Nate to strap on the riot gear for a simple patient escort, Nate was naturally worried.

Ten minutes later, they were equipped with enough gear to stop the Chicago riots and waddling down the corridor of the infamous Block C. The block was full of lifers. Every single patient in the notorious block was considered to be truly unredeemable and absolutely under no circumstances to ever be rereleased back into society. They were the maddest of the mad. Not even Folsom or San Quentin wanted the Block C maniacs.

It was quiet. Nate thought that made it worse. Somehow, it was scarier when the truly mad were quiet. If they weren't yelling and screaming, he figured they were thinking, planning, and scheming.

Nate and Beans came to a stop outside of room C12. Beans had a master key on a chain around his neck. He gripped it awkwardly in his gloved hands while Nate held the baton in his hand.

Beans's fingers shook as he slid the key into the lock one groove at a time, nice and slow and considered. Before he turned the key and opened the door to reveal whatever evil was on the other side, he looked back over his shoulder at Nate. "If anything happens," he said, "don't hesitate to crack a skull or two."

Nate tried to swallow, but his mouth was dry, so he just held on to the baton and hoped for the best.

Beans turned the key and pushed open the door. The room was dark except for where the hot Texas sun blasted through a small window, shining a light on the sole occupant of room C12. Nate had expected Ted Bundy, Charlie Manson, and Mr. T all rolled into one. What he hadn't expected was the girl.

She couldn't have been more than twenty-five-years old, not much over five feet seven, and no reasonable person would have assumed she was much of a threat by just looking at her. She brushed the mop of blond hair away from her face, saw Nate and Beans in their riot gear, and smiled.

"A little overdressed, aren't you, boys?" Parker Ames asked.

THREE

DR. JEREMIAH ELLIS HATED ASYLUMS. He hated
hospitals, and most of all, he hated the sterile disin-
fectant smell they all had in common. Unfortunately,
no matter how much he would like to, he couldn't
work out of his private practice in Fort Worth all the
time. He spent the majority of his day traveling all
over Texas, visiting hospital after hospital, inter-
viewing and treating the mentally deranged—people
his ex-wife called "the loons."

He'd never quite let go of the '60s and believed
everything could be solved with love, understanding,
and sometimes a healthy dose of LSD. He was the
first professional in the industry to treat murderous
psychopaths as real people with real feelings, but it
wasn't until after his book, *Bloodbath at Miss Kitty's:
The Exploration of a Psycho Killer*, was published in

1978 that he became a household name. He'd written the book during a two-week Benzedrine frenzy at the tail end of a six-month research trip in the wake of a mass murder in Huntsville, Tennessee.

For forty years, Miss Kitty ran Miss Kitty's Boarding House, giving refuge to thousands of weary souls cutting across the country from one side to the other. As far as anybody knew, Miss Kitty was a sweet old lady famous for her lemon pies and easy smile. What most people didn't know until much, much later was that behind closed doors, Miss Kitty was not only one hell of a baker, but she was also a serial killer.

Over the course of forty years, it was estimated that Miss Kitty disposed of over three hundred unsuspecting poor souls. Given the transient nature of the boarders at her house, it wasn't uncommon for people to travel into town, stay a night or two, and travel on back out… or not. In a lot of the cases, moving on was exactly what they did. But in some of the cases, something much darker took place.

In the winter of 1927, Miss Kitty's father, Ezekiel Kitty, purchased a two-story nine-room house on the corner of 11th and Normal Park and converted it into a boarding house. It took all the money her father had saved up over years and years to purchase the boarding house, and with seven mouths to feed, he damn well needed to make the business work. And for a couple of years, it worked just fine. That was until the Great Depression hit.

Depression or not, there were still people who needed a place to flop; that was for sure. But the money they had to spend had dried up, and Ezekiel found that he needed to drop the prices so low that it was like they were getting robbed. Those seven mouths were still hungry mouths, and Ezekiel found it was becoming close to impossible to put food on the table. That was until it occurred to him that meat was meat.

He didn't see what he was doing as murder; he saw it as survival. The Kitty children never went hungry again.

Ezekiel Kitty died in the winter of '49. The brothers and sisters moved away and that left the third daughter, Penelope Kitty, to run the boarding house and keep food in her belly.

Dr. Ellis had always thought the title, *Bloodbath at Miss Kitty's: The Exploration of a Psycho Killer*, was misleading. Miss Kitty hadn't created a bloodbath exactly; it was more like a slow drip over a number of years. Then there was the "exploration of a psycho killer" part of the title. Was there something deeply wrong about Miss Kitty? Absolutely in Dr. Ellis's professional opinion, she was all kinds of broken inside, but Dr. Ellis couldn't say with absolute certainty that she was a psycho killer. He could argue that she lacked a conscience, that she lacked empathy, and that she had little regard for human life, but was she a psychopathic killer? He had concluded that she wasn't psychopathic at all. She was very much aware of her actions and the consequences. She simply just liked the taste of human flesh.

"I never killed more than I ate," Miss Kitty had said at her sentencing.

Despite the misleading title, the non-fiction book had hit the bestseller charts within weeks and catapulted Jeremiah Ellis into the celebrity spotlight. He went on all the talk shows, became an expert on the subject, and even briefly dated Sally Jessy Raphael. But that was ten years ago, and in those years since, Ellis's star had faded. People recognized him occasionally, but whenever they did, it was like they weren't quite sure from where or for what.

When the door to the interview room opened, Ellis put his cigarette out in the ashtray, stood up and watched as Parker Ames was wheeled in. The guards weren't taking any chances. They had strapped her ankles and wrists to the wheelchair, and she had a muzzle over her face as if she were some sort of wild animal. All he could see were her blue eyes peeking out between her locks of blond hair. He didn't need to see much more to know that she wasn't exactly impressed with her current situation.

Ellis sat back down and shifted his gaze from Parker to the guards and back to Parker. Clearly, the guards weren't going to leave, and a part of Ellis was grateful for that.

Carefully, he unpacked his briefcase and laid the contents on the table. Parker's file was four inches thick, and he had lost track of how many times he had read it. But every single time, he hoped that he would find a little clue or an answer as to not only what had happened, but more importantly, why it had happened.

He took his pen out of his shirt pocket, placed it near the folder, and looked back up at Parker. "It's been a long time."

"Armrumamaumarum," Parker said. It was impossible to understand a word through the muzzle.

He leaned forward. "I beg your pardon?"

"Armumumerumarum."

Ellis looked at Beans. "I can't conduct an interview like this. Can we take the mask off?"

"I'm not sure you want to do that, Doc," Beans said.

"Can we just do it?"

He unstrapped the muzzle from the back of Parker's head, and the first thing—the *very* first thing—she did was spit clear across the table into Dr. Ellis's face.

Beans gave him a look as if to say, "I told you so." But Ellis took it like a trouper and wiped his face with a handkerchief from his pocket.

"Parker," he said, ignoring her previous indiscretion, "I'm here to assess whether or not you should be released from this institution."

"You want to know if I've been a good girl."

"Something like that."

"I really can't say with any certainty that I have."

Ellis picked up his pen, put the end between his teeth, and leaned back in his chair. "Tell me about your mother."

"I'd rather not."

"All right," he said. "Tell me about your father then."

She raised an eyebrow. That wasn't going to happen either.

Ellis put the pen down. He was getting nowhere. "Indulge me."

"I don't really feel in an indulging kind of mood."

"If you want any chance of getting out of here, you're going to need to answer some of my questions."

"I didn't kill them, you know? My parents."

"Then who did?"

"If I told you…" Parker said. "If I told you the truth without any embellishments, exaggerations, or lies, you wouldn't believe a single word of it."

Ellis lit a cigarette. "Try me."

FOUR

THE YEAR WAS 1978 and back then, Parker Ames was nothing more than a typical sixteen-year-old girl who thought the idea of supernatural unkillable slashers running around the country murdering people was as ridiculous as the idea of Van Halen breaking up.

At that age, Parker Ames was rather unremarkable. She was daughter of Raymond and Annie Ames, and they lived in a two-story house in a little town called Chesterton in Northern Indiana. Raymond was a chemist at a research facility in Valparaiso. Annie worked part-time as a real estate agent and spent the rest of the week volunteering at their local church. They had a good life. They weren't rich, but they never worried about money either, and by all accounts, their little part of the world was plodding along just as it should have been. Everybody was healthy, and everybody was happy.

All that changed one Friday night in late July.

Parker was upstairs in her room, listening the new Blondie album she'd borrowed from Casey Hill, who was in her American History class. She was three songs in and already knew it was going to be her album of the summer. Her parents had already given her an advance on her allowance to buy a pair of Chuck Taylors, so she would have to wait at least two weeks to get her hands on her very own copy of it. Until then, she was going to burn every single note, lyric, and sound into her head over the weekend before she gave that record back to Casey Hill.

What she didn't know was that at that very moment, her father was behind the wheel of their Ford Squire station wagon with blood on his face and a shake in his hands. Somewhere along the way, he had lost his glasses, and keeping the car on the road took all his concentration.

A wave of relief washed over him as he spied the blurry view of their house up ahead. The station wagon bounced up and over the sidewalk as it came to a stop in the middle of their neatly trimmed lawn. Ray swung open the car door. He was still wearing his laboratory coat from SP research, and just like his face, it too was covered in blood.

"Is everything okay?" their neighbor, Diana Leigh, asked from her side of the fence. She was out watering her garden as she thought the plants drank more water in the evening hours than the day and, therefore, always did her watering at night.

"Everything's just fine," Ray said, trying to keep his voice measured.

"Is that blood?" She motioned to the splatter on his shirt.

Ray didn't answer. The front door was unlocked. He pulled it open, went in, locked the door, and went straight into the kitchen, where he knew Annie would be making dinner.

She heard him come in and was halfway through asking how his day was when she turned and saw the blood and the panic on his face. "What happened?"

He grabbed her by the shoulders, and his blood-shot eyes stared straight into hers. "We have to go," he said. "We have to go now."

She laughed and shook him off, hoping it was a joke. "What are you talking about?"

"It went bad," he said. "The experiment today, it went real bad."

Annie went white. She almost didn't want to ask,

but she eventually mustered up the courage. "How bad?"

He struggled to find the words, but there really weren't any to describe the horror he'd seen. "He's coming," Ray said. "He's coming for all of us." And it was the second time he said it that made the hairs on Annie's neck stand up.

"Get the shotgun," she said. "I'll get Parker."

And that's exactly just what they did. She headed upstairs, and he rushed to the basement. It was a mess down there. Annie was always on his back about cleaning the basement out and rearranging all the boxes and old furniture, but after a full, busy week at work, the last thing Ray could be bothered doing was getting down into the basement and having to make sense of fifteen years' worth of junk. He'd put it off, Annie had grown tired of asking, and the junk had accumulated as the years passed. He stumbled over an old couch, a box, and some of Parker's old toys, and in that moment, he wished he'd listened to Annie. He made his way through the mess to the gun cabinet and hit the combination dial lock. Ray knew the numbers. He had known them his whole life. The cabinet had been his father's, and his father was an avid hunter who had gone shooting every single weekend since as far back as Ray could remember. He'd tried to entice his son into the sport, but Ray wasn't much for shooting, and eventually, they'd found other hobbies to bond over.

After his father's death, Ray inherited the cabinet and his father's collection of rifles and shotguns. He had no need for them and figured that somebody might as well get some enjoyment out of them, but when it came to selling his father's favorite shotgun, Ray just couldn't bring himself to sell it. Given the current situation, he was glad he hadn't.

He spun the dial: 14 to the left, 6 to the right, and 9 to the left.

Locked.

Shit! He tried again—14 to the left, 6 to the right, and 9 to the left.

Locked.

He dried his sweaty hands on his pants, took a breath, and tried again. The numbers were correct. He was just rushing them—that's all.

Ray turned the dial—14 to the left. 6 to the right, and 9 to the left.

The cabinet door clicked open, and Ray pulled out his father's shotgun and a box of shells. It had been twenty years since he had fired a gun, but he figured it wasn't exactly something that a person forgets. It wasn't exactly like he had a choice at that point in time anyway.

He loaded it up, shell after shell until it was fully

loaded, then he racked the Remington and headed back through the rubble and back up the stairs.

He could hear Annie upstairs. She must have been moving around packing a bag. In five minutes, they would be out of the house, in the car, and safe. SP Research would clean up the whole mess, and everything would go back to normal. All they needed was to survive the next five minutes. With his father's shotgun in his hand, Ray took a breath and allowed himself to think that maybe, with a little bit of luck, they would survive Hurricane Williams.

What Ray didn't know was that Hurricane Williams was standing right behind him.

FIVE

ANNIE CALLED OUT TO PARKER. She told her to get her ass up, pack a bag, and go downstairs. Then she went into her bedroom, dragged a suitcase out of the wardrobe, tossed it up onto the bed, and randomly threw clothes inside. Usually, Annie was a gold-star packer. She could pack a week's worth of clothes into an overnight bag. It was all about how the items were placed to maximize the space. It took time and thought—neither of which Annie had at that particular moment. Nothing in the bag matched, and she didn't care. The only thought she gave was to pack liberal amounts of underwear and socks. She didn't know how long they would be gone or where they were going, let alone whether or not there would be a washing machine when they got there, wherever *there* was. All she did was throw clothes in as fast as she could.

"Parker!" she called out again, and in all the rushing and calling, she realized that she hadn't heard Parker call back once. It wouldn't have been the first time Parker had ignored her mother, but her daughter wasn't the kind to ignore her when she had a tone in her voice. And she knew that she had a tone in her voice because she could hear it. That tone was fear.

She called out one more time, and when she didn't hear anything, she stepped out into the hall, made her way down the hall, and wrapped her fingers around the doorknob to Parker's room.

SIX

THE DOOR SWUNG OPEN.

"Parker! Now!" Annie said.

But Parker couldn't hear a word. She was lying on her bed, flicking through pages of *Rolling Stone*. Her headphones were on, and she had Blondie's *Parallel Lines* blasting so loud that even Annie could hear every single lyric and note.

"Parker, would you please take those—"

Hurricane Williams emerged from the darkness behind her. He stood motionless for a brief second then suddenly, he grabbed hold of Annie and dragged her out of the doorframe.

Parker didn't hear a sound. She just bopped away on her bed, her toes tapping and head rocking away to Debbie Harry's voice. Even though Parker couldn't hear them, there *were* sounds coming out of the Ames household—awful sounds.

There were screams. Some were short, some were long, and others were silenced by a blow or two. The walls shook as Annie slammed into them.

There were sounds of flesh pounding flesh to silence those cries, and still, Parker didn't hear a thing. Little by little, the screams quietened to sobs. The beating and pounding grew less intense, and not too long after that, there was just plain old-fashioned silence.

For a moment, the only noise was tinny excess sound leaking out of Parker's headphones. Then there were the footsteps, and a moment later, Hurricane stepped into the room, barely fitting in the doorframe.

He stepped to the edge of the bed, with a machete in his hand. He raised it high over Parker, and then just as he was about to slam it down, Parker turned at the very last second, and saw the great, big hulking nightmare above her. And of course, she screamed.

Hurricane swung and slammed that machete down, but just as he was about to tear Parker in two, she rolled off the bed, and the machete buried itself into the mattress.

Within seconds, Parker was on her feet. She took

one look at the slasher and another at the door. She didn't have to think twice about making her next decision. She ran.

Parker didn't make it far. On the floor in the hall was her mother's mangled corpse, and the sight of it stopped her dead in her tracks. She dropped to her knees and brushed the bloody hair out of Annie's face. "Mom…"

But there was no point. Annie was gone.

Then Hurricane stepped into the hall. He was right on her tail, and there wasn't much time to stick around.

Parker looked back at the slasher and had two thoughts: *1) What the fuck is going on?* and 2) *Run.*

The second was exactly what she did. She hit the stairs and bounced down them three at a time until she was in the living room, and as soon as she was there, Parker froze with her hands over her mouth and screamed. At her feet was the disjointed body of her father on the floor. Every bendable part had been bent in the wrong direction. Raymond Ames was one horrific mess.

"Parker…" he said. The poor bastard was still alive.

Parker didn't know what to do. She wanted to help him but didn't want to hurt him any further, so she just stood there.

"Parker," he said again in barely a whisper. "Run."

In shock, she didn't budge an inch.

Then with whatever energy, he had left he called out again, louder this time, "Run!"

Hurricane's footsteps thumping down the stairs broke her out of the trance.

That was it! Time to get the hell out of there. Parker tried for the door.

No good! The son of a bitch was locked.

She turned, ready to make a run for the back door, but she was shit out of luck. Hurricane was blocking the only other exit.

Parker considered her options. "I suppose if I ask nicely, you're probably not going to move, are you?"

He shook his head very slowly.

"I didn't think so." Parker tried to make a run for it, but the slasher grabbed her by the hair and threw her clean across the room. She hit the wall hard and slumped to the floor.

Before she had a chance to climb to her feet, Hurricane picked her up and threw her against the other wall as if she were a rag doll.

Parker was beat. She got to her hands and knees and spat blood. She tried to get up but didn't have the energy. She looked over at the slasher. There was one thought and one thought only on her mind.

"Why?" she muttered.

He wasn't a talker and didn't say a word. He came in for the final blow, the death blow. It was almost the end of the line for Parker…

Then she saw something out of the corner of her eye—a shotgun. Her father's shotgun. With her last ounce of energy, she reached out, wrapped her fingers around the stock, swung the barrel toward Hurricane, wrapped her finger around the trigger, and squeezed.

Bam! She unleashed a shell into him. It didn't put him down, but with renewed energy, Parker climbed to her feet, racked the shotgun, and… *Bam!*

Another round.

And then another and another after that.

Bam!

Bam!

Bam!

Each blast sent him back farther and farther out of the room, until he hit the floor in the kitchen. He was out for the count, and the fear and anxiety in the room dropped down a notch or two. The shotgun slipped from Parker's fingers, and she drew in a long deep breath.

Fucked was the most appropriate word to describe Parker Ames in that very moment. Without the energy to do much more, she dropped to her knees and wailed.

She cried as one thousand emotions ran through her body all at once. The sound of her cries bounced off the walls and come back at her, making it sound as if she weren't the only one wailing in the night. She gasped for air, and it was only then that she heard the sound of the police sirens fading up in the distance. They would be there in a few moments, and she knew she would have to explain to them what had happened. How could she explain this? She didn't even know what had happened. In the space of ten minutes, her entire world had changed.

Then she heard a shallow voice. "Parker," her father said.

She didn't even want to look at him, but she knew she had to. So when she did look at her father, she stared straight into his eyes and not at the brokenness of his body.

"Your mother?" he asked.

Parker couldn't bring herself to say the words, so she just shook her head, pushing back the tears.

Raymond closed his eyes and took in a painful breath.

"I'll call an ambulance," she said.

"No."

"They'll fix you up."

He motioned as best he could at his mangled body. "Let me be with your mom."

"What?"

"You can do it," he said. "I need you to do it."

"Do what?"

His hand of broken fingers reached out and pointed at the shotgun.

"Dad, no," she said.

"Please." His voice was starting to slur. "I don't want to live like this."

Parker made herself look at him. Really look at him. At his disjointed and broken body. At the bones poking out of the flesh. At how his limbs were bent in directions they should never be bent. Parker wiped the tears from her eyes and slowly rose to her feet with the shotgun in hand.

"It'll be okay," he said.

"No, it won't," she said as she leveled out the shotgun and took aim at her old man. "None of this is okay." Her finger wrapped around the trigger, she paused.

"It's okay, baby," he said.

Then she squeezed the trigger. The blast echoed throughout the house, then everything fell silent again. Parker closed her eyes and drew in a deep, shaky breath. When she opened them again, a tear rolled down her cheek. She remembered her dad teaching her to ride a bike. She remembered him holding her when she was scared. And she remembered him every Christmas Eve, when he pretended to be Santa Claus and Parker pretended to not know it was him.

Then as if she'd just remembered something, her eyes snapped to the kitchen. Hurricane Williams was gone!

When the police turned up, the flashing red and blue lights bounced off her face as she stepped out of the house and onto the veranda. The two uniforms had their weapons set to rock 'n' roll, but they stopped dead in their tracks when they saw Parker covered in blood.

"Miss," one said, "are you okay?"

"What do you think?" she replied.

The cops lowered their weapons; they didn't know what the hell else to do but stare.

SEVEN

LATER ON THAT NIGHT, after the detectives, para-
medics, and reporters all arrived, Parker sat on the
back of the ambulance by herself and watched as the
body bags containing her mother and father were
carried out of the house, which would be known for
years as Hell House by the local kids. She wrapped
the blanket a little tighter around her shoulders, dug
her fingers into the pocket of her jeans, and pulled
out a crushed packet of cigarettes. She set one on fire
with her shaky hands, pulled a lungful of smoke into
her lungs, then slowly let it escape from her nostrils.

None of it felt real to her. The house didn't feel
like her house anymore, and the people in the body
bags didn't feel like her parents anymore. It was as if
she were watching a movie. And not even a good
movie. The movie she was watching was something

that played on late-night television or in grungy drive-ins on the outskirts of town. The kind of place teenagers only went to so they could make out. It wasn't her life. It was just a bad movie. That was what she tried to tell herself anyway, but no matter how many times she repeated that in her head, she knew it wasn't true. It was her house. The bodies in those body bags were her parents, and the blood on her hands was theirs.

The life she had yesterday was nothing more than a fading memory. Over time, it would corrode and be forgotten like rain on a window.

She would never have another birthday party. She would never have another Christmas. She would never be able to call her mom when she needed to call her mom. Her father would never walk her down the aisle. Her children would never have grandparents. All she felt was anger over a future lost and thrown on another track, because if she knew one thing and one thing only, Parker Ames knew she was going to find the son of a bitch who'd destroyed her family. Then she was going to tear him apart piece by bloody piece.

She just didn't know where to start. Parker killed the cigarette under her Converse just as a pair of headlights emerged from the darkness. As they neared, the chug, chug, chug of the V8 grew, then the muscle car came to a stop in the middle of the street outside the house. At four in the morning, the crime scene was quieter than it had been a few hours ago. The reporters had left, the neighbors had gone back into their homes, and the army of uniforms that had been sent to the house had all been reassigned after searching the area and determining that Hurricane Williams had fled and was probably miles away by then.

The V8 sat silent for a moment. Parker peered forward to see who was behind the wheel, but all she could see was the reflection of the moonlight on the windshield. Then the door opened and closed, and at first, Parker saw the driver only in fragments.

She saw the alligator cowboy boots.

She saw the blade strapped to their thigh.

And she saw the eye patch.

It wasn't until she put all those pieces together that she saw Delores McCormick in all her badass entirety. She must have been in her forties, but she looked as if she had lived twice that long, consid-ering the attitude and scars she carried with her. She was five foot eight, tops. Her hair was black and short, and her one eye was dark brown. She wore leather pants and a leather jacket and was a cross somewhere between Joan Jett and Kurt Russell.

McCormick knew where she was heading and

made a beeline for Parker. "Is that bastard dead?"

Parker cocked her head at that strange woman. "Dead-ish."

"Did you take his head?"

"What?" Parker asked, confused as all hell.

"If you didn't take his head," McCormick said, "then he's still out there. The question is, dear girl, what are you going to do about it?"

"Me?"

McCormick crouched to get eye to eye with Parker. "You can be a victim, or you can come with me," she said. "If you come with me, I guarantee that I will teach you how to kill every last one of these motherfuckers."

Parker didn't even give it so much as a second thought. She climbed to her feet, tossed the blanket into the back of the ambulance, and followed McCormick back to the muscle car. Once Parker had climbed inside, they hit the road.

"You're probably wondering who the hell I am, aren't you?" McCormick said, changing gears.

"The thought was on my mind."

"And you're probably wondering what the hell that thing was back at your house."

"That does seem to be a bit of an unanswered question."

McCormick thumbed back at the house. "It was a

slasher."

"A what?"

"A slasher," she repeated. "Not a vampire, not a werewolf or a psycho killer, but a slasher."

"You're fucking kidding me, right?"

"Did you put a bullet in him?" McCormick asked.

"Two."

"And how did that work out for you?"

"He got up and left."

"They tend to do that."

Parker leaned forward. "They?"

"He's not the only one."

"There's more of those things?"

"There are."

"What are they?"

"Sometimes, a man is so evil that not even hell will take him. They stay here, and they hunt and kill. In short, they're a real goddamned pain in the ass."

"And you hunt them?"

McCormick smiled. "And you will too."

It turned out that Delores McCormick had been hunting sons of bitches like Hurricane Williams all her life. She'd killed her first slasher when she was seven years old. Then when she was sixteen, she took out the infamous Twin Pines killer, and by the time she was in her twenties, McCormick had personally fucked up over thirty slashers in a dozen countries.

You see, Delores McCormick came from a long line of hunters. Her mother hunted them during World War II. Her grandmother hunted them in during the Industrial Revolution, and her mother before her beheaded over fifty slashers all across Europe. Beheading sons of bitches was the family business, and by all accounts, business was good. From mother to daughter, skills, knowledge, and history were passed down, and for hundreds of years, those women kept evil at bay.

But in a cruel twist of fate while battling the Preacher in Alabama, McCormick fell off a church onto a picket fence. She managed to ram one of those pickets through the Preacher's face, but the damage she sustained from the fall almost killed her. She was rushed to New Light Medical, and in an emergency procedure that saved her life, Dr. Ferzetti removed her uterus. He'd saved her life, but Delores McCormick would never be a mother. So if she died, which, given her profession, was very likely, then every single little piece of information that had been passed on down to her from her mother and her mother's mother would be lost to the world. Slashers would rise, and death would engulf the world.

Delores McCormick needed an apprentice, and the recently orphaned Parker Ames was the perfect candidate.

EIGHT

ON THE OUTSKIRTS OF DETROIT, not far from the old Wayne County Jail, was an industrial park where Lincoln used to make the Continental. They didn't make the Continental there anymore, and all that was left were the empty factories the company hadn't been able to sell off when they went under. Creditors owned those factories, and given the current state of disrepair the structures were in, it was clear they didn't know what do with the buildings. So they sat on the outskirts of the JB Subdivision, empty, quiet, and alone… except for one warehouse on Burns Drive.

Five years ago, it had housed engine parts and mufflers. All that stock had been used, sold off, or transported to another warehouse to service another factory. In the summer of 1988, though, it was used for another purpose altogether.

Parker stood over a bench and ran her eyes over the collection of slasher-hunting weapons laid out on it. There were a handful of rusty machetes, a blood-stained chain saw, a few butcher knives, one power drill, an ax, a pitchfork, and an assortment of blades, hammers and other blunt instruments. It was two weeks after the events at Hell House, and Parker had cleaned up and was standing there in her gym gear, ready to learn how to get her revenge. McCormick motioned to the table and the horrendous weapons on it. "These are your basic slasher weapons. You get caught with your back against the wall, you're going to want to have one of these bad boys in your hands. This is the only tool kit a final girl will ever need."

Parker picked up a machete and was admiring it in her hand when she heard a groan echo throughout the warehouse. "What the hell was that?"

McCormick took half a dozen steps toward a shark cage with a sheet draped over it and yanked it off to reveal a filthy slasher dressed in a tattered Santa costume with a bloody pillowcase over his head.

"Who's been naughty? Who's been nice?" he said over and over again with a voice that sounded as if it had been given a once-over with a sander. "Who's been naughty? Who's been nice?"

"What have you done to Santa?" Parker asked.

"This is Billy," McCormick said. "Thirty years ago on Christmas Eve, Billy and his family were traveling along the freeway. They were on their way home from church to enjoy some hot chocolate and open some presents. Then out of the darkness and snow, Billy's father saw a man on the side of the road. His car had blown a tire, and to Billy's father, it looked as if he were trying to change it. So Billy's father pulled the family station wagon over to help the man, like the Good Samaritan that he was. The man in need was dressed as Santa Claus. He was also a raving fucking lunatic. Billy, who was only a little boy at the time, watched his parents get dismembered while the radio played the Christmas carol 'Do You Hear What I Hear?'"

"Who's been naughty? Who's been nice?" Billy said again.

McCormick told him to shut up and continued her story. "Fast-forward twenty-five years later, and Billy's living his life like a well-adjusted human being with a steady job at the local bank, a fiancée, and a bright future ahead of him. Everything was just all hunky-dory, until one Christmas Eve when he's in the homeware section at Macy's, and guess what happened to come on the radio?"

"'Do You Hear What I Hear?'" Parker said.

"That's right," McCormick said. "Something inside of Billy snapped when he heard that song. He murdered eight people that night before the police arrived and shot him dead in the perfume section. They put seven bullets in him, but like all good slashers, the bullets had little effect. Later on, while he was at the morgue, our friend Billy here regenerated, woke up, killed the coroner and his assistant, and disappeared into the Virginia night. I tracked him for three months across half a dozen states. He killed nine more people before I caught up with him."

"And now you keep him around for Christmas cheer?" Parker asked, looking the slasher up and down.

"No," McCormick said. "I keep him around for practice." She unhooked the lock and swung open the shark cage door, and Evil Santa took a couple of menacing steps out.

"What the hell are you doing?" Parker asked as she stepped back.

"You want to fight slashers," McCormick said. "This is a slasher."

He took slow but determined steps toward Parker.

"Can't we work up to this?" she asked.

McCormick shook her head. "Nope."

"I need a weapon," Parker said with panic in her voice.

McCormick motioned to the bench of machetes, blades, and hardware. "Take your pick."

Evil Santa was making the slow and steady pace with one target on his mind—Parker.

"A real weapon. Give me a gun," she said.

"You want a gun?" McCormick asked.

"Yes!" she snapped. "I want a gun."

"Okay." McCormick gripped a 9mm from the small of her back and tossed it through the air.

Parker caught it, took aim at Evil Santa square in the face, wrapped her finger around the trigger, and squeezed.

Bang! Bang!

She put two in his chest, and Evil Santa hit the deck.

Parker threw a cocky smirk McCormick's way. "And that's how it's done.

McCormick crossed her arms. "Is it?"

There was a groan. They both heard it at the same time, and there was little doubt as to where that groan came from. Evil Santa tossed and turned, then the scary son of a bitch climbed to his feet as if nothing at all had happened.

The smirk dropped from Parker's face. She pulled the gun up again, took aim, and…

Bang!

Bang!

She put two more in his chest, and just like before, Evil Santa hit the deck.

There were no more smirks and no more cockiness from Parker—that was for sure. She kept the gun in her hand and her aim on the slasher.

Then… Evil Santa groaned, moaned, and again climbed to his feet. And just like before, he came at her, and with one lunge, Billy the Evil Santa wrapped his fingers around Parker's throat.

"What the fuck!" she snapped, but that was about all she could get out because Evil Santa's fingers were squeezing tight.

"He's a slasher, sweetheart," McCormick said as she slid a machete from the bench and held it in her hand. "And with a slasher, you either take the head, or you go home." With one violent swing, she separated Evil Santa's bloody pillow-cased head from his body and sent it bouncing along the floor.

Parker dropped to her hands and knees, gasping for air. After a couple of deep breaths, she managed to slow her heart beat down, and her mind began to come to terms with what the hell she was dealing with. "They won't die."

McCormick pulled a rag from her back pocket and wiped the blood off the machete as she leaned down to Parker. "Don't be mistaken. They die. Some die a lot harder than others. We don't know why, but if you shoot them, stab them, or beat them, they will regenerate, and they will come back after you. The one thing they all have in common is that if you take their head, they go to hell and never return."

She offered Parker a hand and helped her to her feet. The apprentice patted herself down and regained her bearings. It was in that moment, Parker noticed another shark cage with another sheet over it.

"Who's in there?" she asked.

"Oh," McCormick said. "You're not quite ready for him yet. But you will be." Her eyes hardened. "You will be."

NINE

THE NEXT MORNING, McCormick woke Parker up at five o'clock, and her training began. It started with a five-mile jog, followed by hand-to-hand combat, where McCormick taught her karate and jujitsu. Then in the afternoon was another five-mile jog, as apparently with slashers, there's a lot of running, so cardio is very important. After the jog, it was weapon work, and to a hunter of slashers, anything and absolutely everything could be used as a weapon. McCormick had once sent a slasher right back to hell with a spork. A goddamned spork.

Then in the afternoon, it was time for school.

"If you're in the business of hunting slashers, and we are very much in that business, then there are a few rules a young heroine needs to abide by."

McCormick held up a finger. "Firstly, never under any circumstances read aloud from a demonic book. In the history of reading aloud from a demonic book, no good has every come from it. Secondly, if you're staring into a mirror, never say the name of a slasher five times. Thirdly, if anybody says they'll be right back, chances are, they won't. Which leads me to my next point. If someone suggests you split up, they're probably going to die." Her voice downshifted to something much more serious. "Lastly, never assume the slasher is dead. You can shoot the slasher. Bury the slasher. Chain the slasher to an engine block and drown them at the bottom of Camp Crystal Lake. But unless you behead the son of a bitch, they will always return."

Every single day was like that, and after three weeks, Parker was exhausted.

"Can't we just do this in a *Rocky* montage or something?" she said.

"A what montage?"

"A *Rocky* montage."

"What's a *Rocky* montage?"

"In the movie *Rocky*, Rocky Balboa tries to become a better boxer by doing push-ups, chin-ups, and chasing chickens, and instead of showing you every single little thing he did, they crammed like months of training into a snappy two-minute montage to some inspirational music."

McCormick looked at her like she was an idiot. "No, we can't do this in a *Rocky* montage."

"Can we at least have some inspirational music?"

"No."

And it went on like that for six months. Now, showing you, dear reader, six months of intense training may not be the best use of your reading time. Do you really want to know about how McCormick made Parker throw a machete into a slasher dummy three thousand times before the blade finally struck the dummy in the head? Well, I do not. So let's go with Parker's idea and do this in a montage. Throw a cassette in that tape deck, blast some inspirational music, and let's get into this montage. I recommend "You're the Best" from the 1985 hit movie *The Karate Kid*.

———

PARKER WOKE up in the morning, and she didn't want to get up. She had never been a morning person, and it was cold in Detroit. Nevertheless, Parker climbed out of her cot, stretched her back, slid on her sneakers, and hit the cold Detroit street, where she jogged through the winter fog for five miles.

Back in the warehouse, Parker ran her finger across the various weapons on the workbench, trying to decide which one to choose. She paused at the machete, picked it up, and admired it in her hand.

With that machete in hand, she walked out of the warehouse, across the street, and into the empty lot that was littered with abandoned furniture and trash. She walked up to one of the trees in the lot and lined the machete up to it.

She took aim and swung. *Donk!* The machete got stuck in the tree. She tried to pull it out, but it was buried in there deep. It was going to be a long road— that was for sure.

"The slasher very rarely appears in the daylight," McCormick said. "Everything you can do in the light, you need to be able to do in the dark."

Parker was at a bench with a blindfold over her eyes and a dozen different parts of a chain saw in front of her.

"You've got twenty seconds." McCormick yelled, "Go!"

Parker's hands frantically rushed around and fumbled over the various parts.

"Fifteen seconds!"

She tried putting two pieces together. The wrong pieces. She slipped, dropped them, then tried two more.

"Ten seconds!"

Finally, she got two pieces together. Then a third!

"Five seconds!"

She connected the chain. With just one more piece to go, she was just about to do it—

McCormick slammed her hand on the table. "Times up! You're dead! Do it again!"

PARKER SWUNG the machete into the tree then pulled it out and swung it again and again and again. There were dozens of trees around her, and each and every one of them had the same battle scars from Parker attacking them with a machete.

BLINDFOLDED, Parker assembled the chain saw. She was getting faster.

PARKER HACKED into the tree with the machete. She was getting faster at that too.

—————

AGAIN, Parker assembled the chain saw. Her hands knew exactly what they're doing. Each piece she grabbed connected to the one before it. Quickly and efficiently, she slid the last piece into place, and when she was done, Parker pulled off her blindfold and looked up at McCormick and her stopwatch.

"Sixteen seconds," McCormick said proudly.

—————

OUT IN THE EMPTY LOT, machete in hand, Parker hacked away at a tree.

Hard.

Fast.

There was a big dent in the side. She didn't let up. Parker just kept on hacking. Wood splinters flew around everywhere and floated in the air. There was not much left of the tree, and a couple of big swings was all it took for Parker Ames to take the whole damn thing down. She swung hard and fast, and with a crunch of wood, the tree collapsed to the ground with a thud.

Out of breath and covered in sweat, Parker looked over at McCormick, who gave her the slightest smile of approval.

And with the hacking down of a tree with a machete, Parker Ames had completed the six-month transformation from the scared little girl at Hell House into a slasher-killing machine.

TEN

MCCORMICK WAS out stocking up on supplies when Parker pulled a chair over the cracked concrete of the warehouse and placed it in front of the shark cage with the sheet draped over it. Since Parker's very first day there, that slasher had been kept under wraps. She could hear him, of course. Mostly at night and mostly just groans. For the first week, the noises kept her awake, but six months later, she had grown used to the sounds that would give most people nightmares for eternity.

McCormick had told her not to take the sheet off, and in all the time she had been there, she did what she was told. She obeyed McCormick's order for one simple reason. Seeing another slasher would make it real. Parker remembered little of the night Hurricane Williams had rampaged through her house, and what she did remember was in fragments. That night felt like something she had simply made up, and seeing another slasher would make everything too real. For a long time, she wasn't sure if she was ready for real.

Ready or not, though, she climbed off her chair, took a couple of steps over to the cage, wrapped her hands around the sheet, and yanked it off. The slasher inside was a triple-plus-sized bastard. Literally, he was the size of a refrigerator. And ugly! His face looked like it had been stitched out of a whole bunch of other older, uglier faces.

Parker looked him up and down, from his massive bare feet all the way up his tattered clothes, and settled on his mangled face. "Have you ever considered a mask?"

He didn't even budge. The slasher just stared straight ahead as if she weren't even there. She had to give it to the slashers—they were a patient breed.

Parker was standing there, studying him, when the garage doors opened and McCormick's Camaro cruised in out of the Detroit night. When she climbed out and saw Parker standing in front of the cage, there was no yelling or chastising. McCormick just made her way across the floor and stood shoulder to shoulder with her protégée. For a moment, all the pair of them did was stare down the slasher.

"Ugly motherfucker, isn't he?" McCormick said.

"Probably won't be winning too many beauty pageants, I'd imagine."

"No, I couldn't imagine he would." McCormick spat some tobacco on the ground. "Unless it was an ugly motherfucker beauty pageant."

"Probably not too many of them." Parker lit a cigarette. "Where's he from?"

"Alabama. He's one of the oldest slashers I've ever seen. His name was Anika, but they called him Beast. Not at first, but that was the name he would become to be known as."

"He looks old."

"Over two hundred years old. A little less than two hundred years ago, back when Beast was twenty-two years old and people called him Anika, he was a slave that lived on the Steve P. Vincent plantation. Now the Steve P. Vincent plantation had a reputation of being a somewhat undesirable plantation. Big Daddy Vincent was a particularly cruel man and encouraged that behavior in his overseers. Beatings, rapes, and even the occasional lynching was commonplace on the plantation, and Beast here grew up on that plantation. He wasn't born on some other plantation and sold to Big Daddy Vincent; he was born and bred on the Steve P. Vincent plantation. As a matter of fact, he had never stepped foot off the plantation in all of his twenty-two years. He was always a big boy, but he was also gentle, so people naturally assumed that he was dumb, and naturally, because they assumed he was dumb, they saw him as a non-threat and pretty much left him alone. As long as he picked his fair share of cotton, Anika was free to roam the plantation. There were rules: he had to stay on the grounds, and he couldn't go into the big house. Nobody was allowed to go into the big house. And for his entire life, Anika obeyed those rules. Except for that one time. That's all it took—just once. The story goes he was out the back of the big house, where Big Daddy kept his prized chickens. It was Anika's job to tend to the chickens, and he took the responsibility seriously. So there Anika was, tending to the chickens, which he loved and treated as his own, when Belle—Big Daddy's youngest, and some would say most precocious, daughter—came to the back door. You see, Belle was the kind of young lady that some would refer to as a…" McCormick struggled to find the right word.

"A slut," Parker offered.

"A slut," McCormick repeated. "Precisely. Now, people may not have used that exact word when describing her, but if they did, they wouldn't be far off. Now what Anika didn't know was that Big Daddy had recently denied Belle a trip to Birmingham, and she was looking for a way to get back at him."

"And sleeping with the help was how she was going to do that?"

"Now Anika might have been a gentle soul, but ever since he was sixteen and Belle was thirteen, he'd had a crush on her. So when Belle invited him into the kitchen for a glass of iced tea, he knew he shouldn't have gone, but he went anyway. When she invited him up to her room, he knew he shouldn't have gone, but he went anyway. And when Belle invited him to sit on her bed, he certainly knew that he shouldn't have done that. But he did it anyway. What Anika didn't know was that on the other side of the plantation was a man who, from a distance, vaguely, if you squinted, looked, somewhat kinda like Anika. And this Anika look-alike just happened to jump the fence of the plantation on his way through, and that man was mighty hungry. As he was cutting across the land, he came across Big Daddy's prized chickens and thought to himself, 'Damn, I'm hungry. I'm going take me one of those chickens.' And that's just what he did. Now when Big Daddy found out that one of his prized chickens was missing, presumed eaten, well, Big Daddy, he wasn't too happy about that.

"Big Daddy rounded up his overseers, and they

rounded up Anika, who by that time was back with his people at the rear of the plantation. It had been a while since they had themselves a good old-fashioned lynchin', and Big Daddy thought it was time to set an example. So Big Daddy gathered up everybody on the plantation, including his five daughters, which included his youngest, Belle, and they all gathered around a big oak tree just by the big house. They tossed a rope over one of its biggest branches and slipped a noose around young Anika's neck. Then Big Daddy asked him if he'd killed and eaten one of Big Daddy's prized chickens. Now, of course, Anika knew that he hadn't, but he was no fool. He knew that he couldn't tell Big Daddy that at the time his chicken went missing, presumably eaten, he was bedding the young Belle. If he did, there would be a noose around Belle's neck as well, so when Big Daddy asked for a second time if he had killed and eaten the chicken, Anika looked at Belle and told Big Daddy what he wanted to hear. Two minutes later, Anika was swinging from a rope. A minute after that, he ran out of oxygen, and not long after that, he was dead. "

"Only he wasn't," Parker said.

"Not in the traditional sense anyway," McCormick continued. "In the last gasping-for-air minute of his life, Anika prayed. He didn't pray to be saved; he didn't pray for a quick death. The gentle Anika prayed for revenge, for in his mind and in his heart, he didn't deserve what he got." McCormick circled the cage. "God didn't answer his prayers. But the devil did."

"I assume it didn't end too well for Big Daddy Vincent."

"It didn't end too well for anybody," McCormick said. "Sometime just after midnight, Anika pulled himself out of the grave the other slaves had put him in and walked into the big house with nothing but a hammer in his hand. He went through that house room by room, and he put that hammer through their skulls. Twelve people in total."

"What about Belle?"

"That's just it," McCormick said. "What about Belle? Hers was the last room he reached, and when he did, she was awake. She knew what was happening. She hid under the bed, but it wasn't the best hiding place, you see. Anika found her, and when it came time to split her skull in two like everybody else's in the house, Anika just couldn't do it."

"He let her go?"

"He did," McCormick said. "Curious behavior for a slasher. If Anika had left his bloody rampage right there on the Steve P. Vincent plantation, then he and I wouldn't have any problems." McCormick turned to the cage. "But you didn't, did you, Beast? No, you took your show on the road. Southern gentlemen disappeared all over the South for a couple of hundred years. He tore them apart limb by limb and earned himself the nickname of Beast." McCormick shifted her attention back to Parker. "Not all slashers started out as evil. The vast majority of them were turned evil by people who thought they were good."

"It doesn't matter how many of these things we kill. They're just going to keep coming and coming, aren't they?" Parker asked. "What we do isn't really going to matter in the end. Not as long as there's evil in the world, and I figure there's always going to be evil."

McCormick rolled up the sleeve on her left arm to reveal rows of skull-and-crossbones tattoos just like the kind on the fuselages of World War II planes. "I have one for every slasher I've taken down." Then she rolled up the sleeve on her other arm, where she had an elaborate tattoo of a vine full of leaves. "And a leaf for every life I've saved."

There were many, many more leaves than skulls.

"What we do matters," McCormick said.

ELEVEN

PARKER ROLLED over and sat up in her cot. It was the middle of the night, and the warehouse was deathly quiet. She couldn't quite put her finger on it, but Parker knew that something just wasn't right. Moonlight poured through the windows and sent shards of light beaming into the darkness. There was no wind in the air and no distant sounds of traffic and police sirens.

She hung her bare feet over the edge of the cot, quietly planted them on the floor, and pushed herself up as she scanned the warehouse for anything out of the ordinary. The Camaro was exactly where had left it. She saw the machetes, knives, and chain saws on the bench, exactly where they had left them, and then she looked to the shark cage to find that

Beast was absolutely not exactly where they had left him.

The door was open, and he was gone.

Shit, Parker thought. *Shit, shit, shit.*

She looked at McCormick's cot; she was gone. McCormick had trouble sleeping, and it wasn't uncommon for her to spend half the night walking, but unless she had taken Beast for a run, Parker had a problem on her hands.

She shrugged off grogginess from the sleep she was in thirty seconds earlier and headed straight for the weapons. The first one her fingers wrapped around was a chain saw she had named Aerosmith. With a weapon in hand, she felt marginally better, but it was the tiniest of margins.

Parker scanned the room. Beast was nowhere in sight.

Fuck.

Fuck.

Fuck.

Her heart pounded, and sweat rolled down her cheek. "You got this… sure. No problem," she whispered to herself.

She had been training for this. For six months, she had been punching, and rolling, and stabbing, but aside from Hurricane Williams, Parker Ames had never faced a slasher all by herself. And when it came to Hurricane, he had damn well almost killed her.

I should run, Parker thought. *I should run and get the hell out of here. Climb in behind the wheel of the Camaro and get the hell out of Dodge. See you later, Detroit.*

She thought of her mother and father, and then she pushed that thought clear out of her mind.

There was a groan in the darkness, then the absolutely gigantic slasher stepped out into the moonlight.

"Oh, hi," Parker said. "Have you lost weight?"

Weight must have been a touchy subject, because Beast charged at her as if he was in the horror Olympics.

Parker pulled the cord to crank up the chain saw. *Zip! Zip! Zip!*

Aerosmith wouldn't start!

"Shit."

Beast was still coming at her.

She took step back and quickly glanced over her shoulder. Right behind her was an open shipping container—absolutely the very last place Parker wanted to be trapped in with a slasher and a defective chain saw. She yanked the cord again. *Zip! Zip! Zip!*

"Oh, for fuck's sake."

Getting ready to swing, Beast raised his ax when he was only a half a dozen steps away.

Zip! Zip! Zip! Zip! Zip! The son-of-a-bitch chain saw wouldn't kick in.

Beast was on her. He swung.

Parker was almost mincemeat, but at the very last second, she ducked and rolled. Just like McCormick had trained her to do. Six months of hard work and training turned into instinct. She could do this. Maybe she could really do this…

When Parker ducked out of the way, the hulking bulk of Beast couldn't slow down in time. Beast ran straight past her and into the open shipping container. He disappeared into the darkness of it. Parker climbed to her feet and smiled, then when she yanked on the chain saw cord, Aerosmith finally roared to life.

"Got you now, you son of a bitch," Parker said as she moved in with Aerosmith dangling down low, and when the edges of it tapped the concrete, sparks flew. Half a dozen steps later, she disappeared into the darkness of the shipping container.

For a moment, everything was quiet. Not a sound or a whisper. Nothing but absolute silence. Then there was a grunt… the sound of a struggle… and a scream. The chain saw roared, then there were sparks and flashes of light in the darkness. As the battle inside the shipping container raged on, there was movement in another part of the warehouse.

In the darkness, McCormick's figure stepped out from behind the Camaro and into the moonlight streaming in through the windows. There was no concern on her face, and she certainly wasn't in a hurry. She casually made her way over to the container, wrapped her fingers around the handle of the container door, and swung it closed. It hit with a clunk, and when she rotated the big metal arm and pulled it down, the container door was locked with Parker and the slasher inside.

She'd planned whole thing. Every. Last. Single. Detail.

"Hey!" Parker yelled from inside, panic in her voice. "McCormick! Let me out! Let me out! McCormick!"

McCormick didn't budge a muscle. She just stood in front of the shipping container, listening to the brutal fight inside.

TWELVE

THREE HOURS LATER, morning sunlight blasted through the windows of the warehouse. McCormick sat on a stool with a cigarette between her lips. She pulled the smoke back to the butt then crushed it under her foot and left its corpse on the concrete floor alongside all the other butts. The container was quiet, and it had been for hours. McCormick had sat there, listening to the battle that must have been unfolding in near darkness, for close to an hour. It'd escalated dramatically before suddenly falling silent. Then everything was as quiet as a drunken mouse. It was unclear who had survived. Parker or Beast? It really was anybody's guess, and although McCormick hoped Parker had made it, she knew from experience that slashers were a difficult breed to kill. She gave

Parker a thirty percent chance of survival. Hell, even that was generous.

So when McCormick climbed to her feet and made her way over to the container, she didn't have high hopes. McCormick unlocked the door and swung it open.

Sunlight blasted inside. The walls were covered in splashes of blood, and there was Beast, on the floor, minus his head.

Leaning against the wall of the container was Parker with her new best friend, Aerosmith, in her hand. "You're totally out of my cool books," she said when she saw McCormick.

McCormick took a couple of steps into the container, where the inch of blood on the floor rose up around the leather sole of her boots and the thick smell of death hung in the air.

She raised her eyes from the slasher to the brand-spanking-new slasher hunter. "You're ready."

THIRTEEN

EIGHTEEN MONTHS later Parker and McCormick sped through Wessex County, New Jersey, in the Camaro. They made one hell of a team as they traveled from one side of the country to the other, chasing monsters and saving lives. The skull-and-crossbones tattoos on Parker's arm began to grow, and so did the intertwining vines and leaves on the other. Since that long night in the shipping container, the pair of them had taken down twenty-three different slashers, and at that very moment, they were on their way to take down one more.

They barreled past a freshly painted sign: Welcome to Camp Sterling Lake.

"Now this goddamned place," McCormick said. "I've been keeping an eye on this for years. You see, way back in the '50s, it used to be a summer camp, and of course, naturally something horrific happened there, and now the bastard of a joint is haunted by a slasher. In the summer of 1953, a young boy named Clinton Jones attended the camp. He was small and shy and didn't have many friends. His father thought going to the camp would toughen him up, but things didn't really pan out that way. Kids can be cruel and at Camp Sterling Lake, they were particularly cruel. They would steal his clothes when he was in the showers and make him run back to his cabin in front of all the girls. They'd steal his letters that he wrote home, pleading for his parents to come get him, then read them in front of everyone. But the worst of it came when the kids had to go out rowing. Clinton didn't want to go, but the counselor made him. You see, Clinton couldn't swim, but nobody knew that at the time. So when one of the kids knocked him out of the canoe, he kicked and screamed and cried for help, and while everybody pointed and laughed, Clinton slipped under the water. By the time they realized something was wrong, it was way too late. He never resurfaced."

"Never?" Parker asked.

"Well, not straight away. The police came and went. There were searches and divers. But the body of Clinton Jones was never recovered. The camp closed down for the rest of the summer, but the following year, it was business as usual. For a few weeks, everything was fine. The camp counselor ran activities, and everybody seemed to be having fun. That was until one morning when the kids woke up and found that every single counselor was missing. For an entire day, it was a complete mystery. Nobody knew what happened to those teenagers. Then the tide went out, and they discovered what had happened. All ten counselors had boulders chained to their feet, and they were pushed off the pier into the lake."

"They all drowned?"

"And the camp was closed again," McCormick said. "It stayed that way until yesterday, when it reopened."

"You think he's going to come back, this Clinton Jones?"

"Slashers aren't exactly known to let go of a grudge, if you know what I mean."

Thirty minutes later, McCormick slowed the Camaro to a stop at the entrance of the camp. At first glance, it looked like every other summer camp Parker had ever seen, with a dozen or so cabins, a main hall. It was all right by the lake. It was humming and buzzing with kids running around laughing, smiling, and having fun. The place was the perfect hunting ground for a slasher.

"I'll be at the motel a couple of miles down the road," McCormick said. "At the first sign of anything hinky, get on the phone, and I'll be down here in two shakes of a lamb's tail, with a chain saw and a machete."

"Hinky?" Parker repeated with a smirk.

"Yes, hinky. It means…"

"I know what it means. I just never thought I'd hear it come out of your mouth."

"Do you know what else is hinky, young lady?"

Parker's eyes dipped to the floor of the car. "My attitude."

"Exactly," McCormick said. "Now, if you see anything *hinky*, call me, and we'll take him out together."

Parker gave her a nod and climbed out of the car. Instead of the leather and denim battle uniform Parker usually wore, McCormick's young protégée wore a cheerleading uniform. She didn't exactly look comfortable in it either.

Parker leaned back in through the window of the Camaro. "Bye, Mom."

McCormick wasn't having any of it and flipped her the bird. Then she slipped the car into reverse, and Parker watched as she backed out of Camp Sterling Lake. When the Camaro was out of sight, Parker shifted her gaze up to the banner hanging over the entrance of the camp: Welcome to the First National Cheerleading Camp!

"I can't see this ending well," Parker muttered to herself.

Nothing attracted a slasher more than a summer camp. Sex, drugs, booze, and teenagers all rolled into one isolated location made for the perfect prey and the perfect hunting ground. It wasn't Parker's or McCormick's first foray into summer camp hunting. In the previous year, they'd hit up Camp Takago, Camp Timberlane, and Camp Fayette and taken down the three slashers picking off teenagers. They had a pretty good system about it as well. There was no way in hell either one of them could rock up with a chain saw and a machete and tell everyone they were there to go beheading. Nope, they had to be a hell of a lot more subtle.

Generally, Parker would go undercover as a camp counselor and pretend to just be another regular teenage girl with a summer job. During the day, she would she would do activities and chores, but at night, she would patrol the camp, looking for whichever slasher they suspected of being there. It was a good system, and truth be told, it was easy hunting. Any camp where some kid died more or less had something *hinky* going on with it. All they had to do was keep an eye out for camps with tragic histories and take a sharp weapon.

As far as anybody at the camp knew, Parker Ames was Diane Peters from Minnesota. She'd been assigned a bunk in a cabin with four other girls, given a tour of Camp Sterling Lake, and walked through her itinerary for the next upcoming weeks. She had dinner in the main hall, made polite small talk, and pretended that it was *so* exciting to be there.

Later that night, after everybody had gone to bed, Parker lay in her bunk, still fully dressed in her uniform and with a machete right there by her side. She checked the time on her Swatch watch in the moonlight; it was a little after midnight. Parker was going to wait until one in the morning and then go on a patrol to see if Clinton Jones was primed to make a comeback.

When she heard giggling outside the cabin, she rolled over onto her stomach and peered out the window. A handful of girls ran toward the lake. They were obviously up to something that they probably shouldn't have been, which meant that if Clinton Jones was going to make a comeback, a handful of girls sneaking off to the lake the middle of the night was probably as good of a time as any.

Parker rolled off the bunk and gently lowered her feet to the floor. There was a girl in the bunk beneath her, and that girl opened her eyes when she heard Parker. Then those eyes widened when she saw the machete in Parker's hand.

"I'd go back to sleep if I were you," Parker said.

And the girl's eyes snapped closed as if she hadn't seen a thing.

Parker followed the sounds of laughter and fun through the camp and to the lake. She only had moonlight to guide her way, but as she got closer, she saw the scene.

A couple of girls peeled off their clothes and jumped off the pier.

Skinny-dipping. Check.

There were a couple more girls drinking beers with a couple of guys.

Underage drinking. Check.

And over by the woods, there were a couple more naked kids were rolling around.

And teenage sex. Check.

Parker let out a disappointed sigh. "Some people really just asked to be hacked and slashed."

Then there was a scream. It was long, it was loud, and it was full of panic.

Parker's head snapped in the direction of the pier. Clinton Jones stood at the end of it. He was big, bulky and soaking wet. In one hand, he held a fillet knife, and in the other, he held up a cheerleader by the throat. She kicked and struggled, but her feet were far from the ground. No matter how much she kicked and struggled, she wasn't going anywhere. The slasher held that blade up in the air, and within a matter of seconds, he gutted her like a fish.

Naturally, everybody in the vicinity screamed, and really, who could have blamed them? The naked girls gathered their clothes and ran. The guys by the fire didn't skip a beat either, and they, too, took off running. Even the couple in the woods were getting the hell out of there.

Parker stopped one of the girls running past her and pushed a crumpled-up piece of paper into her hand. "Call that number and tell the woman on the other end that Clinton Jones is here and he doesn't like what he sees."

"What are you going to do?" the girl asked.

"Get started early," Parker said as she looked back over at Clinton Jones just as he tossed that poor girl into the lake.

By the time Parker made it down to the pier, the screaming teenagers were all gone, and it was just her and Clinton.

She looked the slasher up and down. "Sorry to break up the party."

Clinton Jones didn't say a word. Slashers weren't exactly chatterboxes.

Over the past eighteen months, Parker Ames had become something close to a samurai with a machete. She could duck and weave her way through any slasher going on the attack. She may have been faster than the slasher and may have been more nimble on her feet, but the truth of it was, in order to go toe to toe with a slasher, she needed to be. The slasher would always have two advantages over her, no matter what. They were always going to be stronger—Parker could hit the weights all day long in the gym, but no matter how many weights she lifted, she would never, not in a million years, be as strong as a slasher. Parker's other disadvantage was that she could stab, slice, and beat up on a slasher all day long, but unless she separated the head from the body, none of it mattered. So when it came down to going into battle, Parker needed to be faster. She needed to not be stabbed, sliced, or beaten along the way… Thankfully for her, she had gotten pretty good at that too.

But not as good as she'd thought.

Parker ran as fast as fast as she could toward the slasher, and with one big kick, he sent her flying back and slamming into the ground. The blow took the wind out of her, and it took Parker couple of deep breaths for her to get herself together. When she did, she climbed to her feet, dusted herself off, and picked up her machete off the ground.

"Okay, you son of a bitch. Let's try that again."

Clinton Jones raised that fillet knife, and Parker knew he was going to throw it—there was no doubting that. Parker knew the body language and exactly what it looked like the very moment a slasher was about to throw a blade. Eighteen months ago, Parker wouldn't have recognized those movements until it was too late. But that was eighteen months ago, and Parker was no longer that little girl from Hell House. So when Clinton Jones pulled his arm back to throw that blade at her, Parker was ready.

She watched as he thrust the blade forward, as it left his fingers, and as it spun through the air. Just as it was about to strike her, Parker ducked.

Somebody who hadn't seen all of those things was Delores McCormick. She didn't dive, duck, or anything, and the knife hit her square in the chest. It took a moment or two for the shock of it to sink in, and when it had, McCormick dropped to her knees and let the chain saw in her hand slip from her fingers.

"That was unexpected," she said.

Parker looked from McCormick to Clinton Jones, and she saw red real fast. She gripped that machete tightly in her hand and charged at the slasher with so much speed and anger that the bastard didn't stand a chance. She swung that machete, and she separated the slasher's head from his body in one swoop and sent Clinton Jones back to hell.

As soon as his body hit the ground with a thud, Parker snapped her head back to McCormick. She was lying on her back, and by the look of it, blood was pumping out of her quickly.

Parker ran back and dropped to her knees. At first, she was shocked by all the blood. She had seen blood before, but this time, it was different. "Come on, let's get you to the hospital."

"No," McCormick managed to say. "I don't think so."

"What? What the hell are you talking about?"

"I'm not going to die in a hospital."

"Would you rather not die at all?"

"It doesn't matter if I get to a hospital or not. We both know I'm not making it out of this one."

Parker gripped her mentor's hand and dipped her eyes to the wound. McCormick was right.

"You can't go," Parker said, pushing back tears. "I don't know what to do."

"Yes, you do." McCormick said. "Kill as many as these bastards as you can."

McCormick drew a breath and closed her eyes. It was the last breath she would ever take.

FOURTEEN

PARKER AMES BECAME the very thing Delores McCormick had hoped she would be: a stone-cold slasher-killing machine. Over the next few years, she sent well over sixty slashers back to hell, and in all that time, she never, not once, laid eyes on Hurricane Williams. It was as if he had just disappeared into thin air.

No matter what she did and no matter how many lives she saved, Parker Ames was still a fugitive on the run for the murder of her parents. And in a small town outside of Cleveland, the FBI finally caught up with her. She had just dispatched a particularly nasty slasher known as the Valpo Hacker and checked into a Motel 6 to have a shower and sleep for a week. Parker's license, bank cards, and plate numbers were all fakes, but they were the best fakes money could buy. She was careful. Parker never slept in the same motel for more than two nights in a row, she never sped, she used all her manners, and there was absolutely zero about her that would raise any law enforcement red flags. So when the FBI knocked on her door with an arrest warrant, all Parker wanted to know was how the hell they'd found her.

Turned out, it was just plain bad luck.

A gas attendant by the name of Pete Daggs had recognized Parker's face from an episode of *Unsolved Mysteries* and called it in. It was that simple. So if Pete Daggs had watched *Cheers* that night instead of *Unsolved Mysteries*, Parker Ames would have been as free as a bird that very moment. Instead, Parker Ames was found guilty of murdering her parents, diagnosed as insane, and committed the Paris, Texas, asylum. The rest, as they say, was history.

Parker's eyes dipped to the papers on the table in front of Dr. Ellis. Along with her file were a bunch of newspaper clippings with various headlines.

"Massacre in Chesterton!"

"Girl Survives Evil!"

"Murderer Loose!"

Parker pulled her eyes up from the clippings to meet Ellis's. "You've got a slasher, don't you? It's Hurricane Williams?"

Ellis closed the folder in front of him. "Why would you say that?"

"No matter how much of a good girl I am, there's not a chance in hell I'm walking out of here. Either he's back, or you have very high hopes for my rehabilitation."

Ellis leaned back in his chair again, rubbed his face, and let out a long sigh. His answer was in those few actions. "There's been a number of murders with similarities to your parents' deaths."

"How many are dead?" Parker asked.

"Two people in Elm Cove, one in Haddonfield, and one in Stall."

Each and every one of those places registered for Parker, and Ellis caught that recognition in her eye. "You know who the next target is, don't you?" he asked.

Parker remained as quiet as a mouse. Her lips were sealed.

He pulled his glasses off and leaned forward. "What's going on here?"

"If you want to stop it, you need to let me out."

Ellis shook his head. "Never going to happen."

"Then we're done here."

After that, she didn't say much. Beans and Nate strapped the muzzle back over her face and wheeled her back to her room on Block C. As punishment for spitting on Dr. Ellis, Beans refused to unstrap her from the wheelchair or take off the muzzle. He told her she needed to get straight and slammed the door on his way out, leaving Parker staring at the brick wall as their footsteps faded down the hall.

She waited until the sun fell from the sky and her little room was washed in darkness. Then for the first time in hours, Parker moved. It wasn't a big move; it was just something slight and small. She turned her left hand around, and in the palm of her hand, she had a pen. Dr. Ellis had carelessly left his pen on the edge of the table, and while the guards were focused on strapping Parker's muzzle back on, she'd extended a couple of fingers, quietly dragged the pen off the table, and made it disappear under palm of her hand. Nobody was the wiser.

She spun it around in her fingers like some sort of rock 'n' roll drummer, looped it under the restraint, and started working it free. A moment later, she was free of the wheelchair restraints, and a moment after that, the muzzle was off her face.

Now all she had to do was get out of that goddamned cell.

FIFTEEN

IT WAS the middle of the night, and the hospital was dead quiet as Doreen Foreman made her nightly rounds through Blocks A, B, and C. Doreen was Texas born and bred. She'd graduated from Saragossa High School and gone to Austin University, and when she'd married her high school sweetheart, they'd honeymooned just over in Hamilton. She had never stepped foot out of Texas, and she was proud of that. It was her seventh night shift in a row, and she was counting down the hours until she could go home, put her feet up, and watch the stories she had taped on the VHS.

Doreen walked the halls of the asylum with a flashlight in one hand and a Newport in the other. The poor souls confined to the asylum were certainly creatures of habit. Every time Doreen did her rounds, she would flash a little light in through the peephole of the door, and every single night, the night owls would be up. Those who watched television were watching television. Those who sobbed themselves to sleep were sobbing, and those who sat in the corner and rocked were rocking. Every night was the same, like clockwork.

When Doreen reached room C9, she flashed her light in the peephole and saw Sandy Downs sound asleep in her bed, just like she always was. Doreen lowered the light and moved on to C10, and when she flashed the light in the peephole, she saw an extreme close-up of Hector on the other side. He was covered in sweat, panting, and only millimeters from the glass, just like he always was. The first time he'd done it, Doreen had almost jumped clean out of her skin, but after a couple of years, she'd gotten used to it.

"Go to bed, Hector," Doreen said. "It's late." And Doreen moved on.

The next room on her list belonged to Parker Ames. Out of all the genuine, certified crazies in the asylum, Parker Ames was the only one that ever gave Doreen the willies. It was simply and overwhelmingly for one reason and one reason only—there was nothing crazy about Parker Ames at all. To Doreen, the young lady in room C11 was just like every other young girl growing up in the '80s. She was smart and pretty, and she had a little bit of a bad attitude. To think of her doing all those horrible things they say she'd done and then act completely normal sent shivers up Doreen's back. She always steered clear of Parker during the day shifts, so at two-thirty in the morning, in the empty and dark halls of the asylum, her contact with Parker Ames was kept to a minimum.

She leaned up to the window and threw a shaft of light into the dark room with her flashlight. Every night for the past twelve months, she'd found Parker asleep in her bed.

But not that night.

Doreen didn't see the girl sleeping under the sheets. In fact, she couldn't find the girl anywhere. Except for the wheelchair and the bed, the room appeared to be empty.

"Hey, Ms. Ames," Doreen said. "I'm not in the mood. Come out where I can see you."

She waited for a reply, but one didn't come. Nothing.

Not.

A.

Single.

Sound.

Doreen banged on the door a couple of times. "Don't make me come in there."

The threat was met with nothing but silence, and after a couple of seconds, Doreen grew impatient. She dug her hand into the pocket of her uniform, pulled out her master key, and unlocked the door.

"You better not be up to anything in here," Doreen said, pushing the door open. She took a careful step into the dark room and panned the flashlight left to right.

"Sorry, Doreen," Parker Ames said as she emerged out of the darkness.

"For what?"

Parker swung a punch, and in one single devastating blow, Parker knocked her the hell out. Needless to say, Doreen hit the deck. "For that."

SIXTEEN

DOREEN'S UNIFORM was a close fit.

A minute later, Parker was in the hall and locking the door to her room, with Doreen on the less sociable side. Parker lit one of Doreen's Newports, pulled back on the first drag, and enjoyed the hell out of it. She had spent the past twelve months in the asylum, and they were quite militant about the rules. No drinking, no smoking, and certainly, under no circumstances whatsoever, no escaping. She was on a smorgasbord of uppers, downers, and don't-make-any-fucking-planners, and they were all designed to keep her in line. Parker had decided pretty early on that staying in line didn't exactly agree with her, so every morning at approximately eight forty-five in the morning, Parker went to the bathroom, got down on her hands and knees, put two fingers down her throat, and blew chunks. Along with her breakfast, the undissolved drugstore that had been administered to her fifteen minutes before under strict supervision, came up.

Parker didn't fancy spending her days in zombie mode.

From a distance and to anyone who didn't look too closely, Parker Ames and Doreen Moore could have passed for one another, and Parker was counting on nobody giving her so much as a second glance. She walked slowly down the corridor with a Newport in one hand and the flashlight in the other—just like Doreen would have. She finished the rounds—just like Doreen would have. And when she was finished, she headed toward the lobby to go on her break—just like Doreen would have.

Beans was in the lobby, sitting at the nurses' station and watching reruns of *The Honeymooners* with a can of Tab and a can of cheese balls between his legs.

If luck was on her side, he would hurry up and have a heart attack right then and there, but Parker figured that was too much to ask for. She was going to have to do it the hard way. So she drew a deep breath, took that first step, and walked with the stride of a woman that had every right to be there. McCormick had always told her that if she did something with enough confidence, people would let her do anything. With that in mind, she aimed her feet toward the double doors twenty feet away that led out to freedom, and she stepped with confidence.

When she reached the door, Parker wrapped her fingers around the handle, and she almost tasted fresh air, when from behind her, way back at the nurses' station, a chair shifted back.

"Hey," Beans called out.

Parker stopped dead, but she didn't dare look back. She was just on pause as a bead of sweat rolled down her cheek and jumped off her chin.

"Yeah," she called back, doing her best impression of Doreen.

"Where are you off to?"

"Gas station," she said. "Gotta get some Newports."

Beans didn't say a word. He just stood, staring at her with his hand on his hips. Sizing her up. Waiting. Watching. Parker thought she was going to have to make a run for it, then just when all hope looked lost, Beans said, "Grab me a 7UP, would you? The machine's all out."

Parker drew a sigh of relief. "Sure. I'll be back in a jiffy."

Beans sat back down, and Parker pushed through the double doors and out to freedom. Her heart felt as if it might pound out of her chest, and it wasn't until she was in the parking lot that it began to slow down. Parker figured she had maybe thirty minutes, tops, until Beans got off his fat ass to find out where the hell Doreen had gone.

She pulled a set of car keys from Doreen's pocket and scanned the parking lot. There was only one vehicle, but what a monster of a vehicle it was: a black 1969 Charger R/T with a massive 440 V8 engine and a hell of a lot of muscle.

"Well, thank you, Doreen."

SEVENTEEN

DR. JEREMIAH ELLIS was awake when the telephone rang a little after two o'clock in the morning. He was on his fifth joint, his third shot of bourbon, and his second listening of the new Simple Minds album. He had lost track of the time, and when he pushed the receiver to his ear he had no idea if it was three in the morning or three in the afternoon. It didn't much bother him either way which it was.

"Yo," he said.

When he heard the voice on the other end and heard what the voice had to say, Dr. Ellis sobered up within seconds. "I'll be right there," he said, jumping out of his La-Z-Boy.

Parker Ames had escaped.

He took a cold shower then brushed his teeth twice to get the smell of pot and bourbon off his breath. Ten minutes after that, he was in his car, speeding down I-82 on his way to the Paris, Texas, mental asylum. He sped from Fort Worth to Paris in ninety minutes with only one stop to gas up and buy a Big Gulp. When Ellis pulled up to the asylum, he expected to see squad cars, police tape, and media vans, but when he brought his red MG to a stop outside the main entrance, he found none of those things. The hospital looked like it did every single other night.

Confusion washed over him as he pushed through the double doors and into the empty foyer. For a moment, Ellis thought that he had smoked too much of the wacky tobacco and imagined the whole thing. For a brief moment, he even thought that maybe he was still back at his house in Fort Worth, sitting on his La-Z-Boy and listening to Simple Minds.

But when he saw Dawkins, the administrator with absolutely the worst comb-over Ellis had ever seen, stomping down the hallway, he knew he wasn't at home listening to Simple Minds, and that Parker Ames really was on the loose.

"Where are the police?" Ellis asked. "Where is everybody?"

"Relax," Dawkins said. "It's not the first time we've had an escape. Security usually finds the patients wandering the grounds by morning. Everything is going to be all right."

"You poor fool," Ellis scoffed. "You have no idea what you're dealing with. This isn't just another patient. This isn't just another one of your drooling idiots. This is Parker Ames we're talking about." Ellis turned on his heels and headed off back down the hall.

"Ellis!" Dawkins called out. "Where the hell are you going?"

"To find Parker Ames and clean up your mess," Ellis said without even so much as a look back over his shoulder.

EIGHTEEN

TEXAS in the height of summer can sometimes be referred to as a miserable, hot son of a bitch, and by noon, a miserable, hot son of a bitch was exactly what Parker called it. Doreen's Charger may have been a monster on the road, but it was all engine and had no bells and certainly no whistles. There was no tape deck or radio, and with the sweltering Texas sun blasting down on the blacktop, the most important thing it was missing was air-conditioning. Even with all the windows down and doing a hundred ten miles an hour, Parker was still drenched in sweat.

She hit the road as soon as she walked out of the asylum, put pedal to the metal, and only stopped for supplies at the mall just outside of Gainesville. Parker couldn't get around in Doreen's uniform without raising too many eyebrows, so when nine o'clock rolled around. she pulled into the Lone Pine Mall and used Doreen's stolen credit card to buy herself a pair of blue jeans, a Save Ferris tee, a leather jacket, and a shovel from Dick's. Within thirty minutes, she was back on the road with a wardrobe change and a cup of hot coffee in her hand.

Parker didn't need any maps; she knew exactly where she was going, and an hour after noon, Parker pulled the Charger off Interstate 277 and onto a dusty road. Anyone speeding past it at one hundred miles an hour could blink and miss it completely—which was exactly what most people did. But not Parker. She had been there many times before.

After ten minutes of driving on the dirt road, she finally eased off the gas and brought the Charger to a stop at the battered and broken Anarchy Cemetery. She climbed out, slipped on the Ray-Bans she'd found in the glove box, and looked over the decrepit graveyard. There couldn't have been more than a hundred gravestones, and all of them were crumbling and overgrown with grass. If cemeteries could die, the Anarchy Cemetery would be exactly how they would look.

Parker popped the trunk and pulled out the shovel, and with that shovel slung over her shoulder, Parker made her way through the maze of gravestones that stuck out of the earth like rows of crooked teeth. She came to a stop at a grave marked "Delores McCormick 1938-1984."

"This will begin to make things right," Parker said, and she slammed the shovel down into the hard soil.

Hours passed. The sun blistered in the sky in shades of orange and red as Parker dug deep into the hard soil, throwing each shovelful over her shoulder and onto the growing mound behind her. It was tough bastard work. The dirt didn't break easily, and when it did, she was lucky if she filled the entire shovel. Parker paused for a moment, wiped the sweat from her brow, and the very next time she slammed that shovel into the dirt, the sound she heard was a dull thud.

Parker smiled. After all that digging, she was finally there. Parker dropped to her knees, cleared the dirt away from the around the edges of the coffin, paused for a brief moment of anticipation, and then opened it up. Inside was a complete arsenal of weapons and instruments designed for pain and horror. She counted 2 Kimber .45s with ammo and holsters, one 12-gauge shotgun with ammo, one set of brass knuckles, one woodsman's ax, one badass machete, way too many knives to count, one hand saw, and most importantly, a custom-built spray-painted-black chain saw that she had named Aerosmith. When Parker picked it up in her hand, it was like greeting an old friend she hadn't seen in ages.

Parker pulled out the yellowed manila folder tucked under a box of ammunition and flipped it open. Inside was a list of names and addresses—a simple list written in black Magic Marker.

ANNIE AMES—DECEASED

RAYMOND AMES—DECEASED

SANDRA KAZAN—DECEASED

MARCIA KURTZ—DECEASED

JUDITH MALINA—DECEASED

SUSAN PERETZ—DECEASED

JENNIFER LANZISERO—DECEASED

LYNETTE SHELDON—DECEASED

ANNA HILL JOHNSTONE—DECEASED

WAYNE SINCLAIR

LIZ SINCLAIR

PARKER AMES

NANCY SINCLAIR

Parker's eyes drilled down on that last name: Nancy Sinclair. Besides Parker's name, she was last one left alive. If Hurricane got to her first, Parker just hoped that Nancy Sinclair knew how to run fast and not trip over.

NINETEEN

PARKER LOADED the weapons from McCormick's coffin into the Charger and hit the road. According to the file, Nancy Sinclair lived at home with her parents in Cedar Springs. It was a two-hour drive from Anarchy, but Parker hammered there in just under an hour. The very instant she hit Nancy's street, she cut her speed to next to nothing and crept the Charger down the road. She kept her eyes peeled as she passed the houses, scanning the yards and windows for Hurricane. All she saw was a teenager doing aerobics in her lounge room, a couple of boys playing baseball in the street, and an old man tending to his roses in his front yard. By all accounts, there was nothing out of the ordinary.

She brought the Charger to a stop outside of 25 Chatsworth Road, shut the engine down, and climbed out of the muscle car. She made her was across the yard and up the couple of steps to the veranda. The Sinclair household was a hundred-year-old two-story home that the Sinclair family obviously loved. In the past couple of years, it had been painted, the veranda that wrapped around the home was tidy and swept, and there was even an American flag doormat that told guests they were welcome.

Parker raised her hand to knock on the door but paused when she saw it was already open a crack. She wasn't the taking-chances kind and unholstered the .45 from her hip. She raised it high and, with her non-shooting hand, slowly pushed open the door and followed the weapon inside. It was a nice suburban home with family photos on the walls, homemade pillows on the sofa, and the smell of cinnamon in the air. The Sinclairs were good people, and it wasn't a stretch for Parker to make that assumption. Sometimes a person could just tell.

Except for the open door, nothing struck her as being out of the ordinary, and Parker was about to holster her weapon and leave when she saw the closed kitchen door and the blood seeping out from underneath it.

It was then that she stopped dead in her tracks.

With her free hand, she gently and very slowly pushed it open. At first, Parker saw the room in small increments. A splash of blood on the toaster. A spray of blood on the wall.

As she opened the door farther, Parker saw the massacre in all its glory. An inch of blood coated the floor, the benches looked as if they had been painted red, and the smell of rust soured the air. The whole joint looked like something out of a Jackson Pollock painting.

But the worst of it were the corpses… or what was left of them. Their limbs had been torn from their bodies and tossed around carelessly. To the regular everyday person, it would have been close to impossible for them to know how many victims there were, but Parker Ames had experience in such things. At half a glance, she knew that there had been two victims: one male and one female, both in their early fifties. Hurricane didn't just want these poor bastards dead—he wanted them ripped apart. Nancy Sinclair wasn't one of the bodies. That meant the girl was still out there somewhere, and he wasn't far behind.

Parker heard a thump outside the kitchen window. She gripped the .45, closed her eyes, and listened. There were more thumps.

Something was out there, all right.

Parker ran through the house, toward the front door, and exploded out onto the veranda, down the couple of stairs, and into the front yard. She was in full battle mode, ready to unleash hell on Hurricane Williams. But rounding the side of the house, she saw a kid running between the fence and the house, and she stopped in her tracks. He was around ten years old, with a baseball cap on backward and a Scorpions tee.

Parker caught up to him, and with a fistful of the back of his T-shirt, she cut his getaway short.

"Hey!" the kid yelled. "Let go of me, lady."

She did, and they both caught their breath.

"Who the fuck are you?" Parker asked.

"Who the fuck are you!" he snapped back.

Parker was a little taken back by the mouth on the kid. "A family friend," she said, chilling out.

"Visit all your friends with a gun, do you?"

"Depends on the friend." Parker holstered the weapon. "What were you doing back there?"

"Taking a shortcut. I was visiting my girlfriend in the next house over. She's got big tits."

"What about the girl that lives here?"

"She's got big tits, too."

Parker clipped him across the head. "Have you seen her?"

"Yeah, I saw her. So what?"

"Where did you see her go?"

He pointed down the street. "Headed that way in her shit-box Nova."

"What's down there?"

"Nothing but Resurrection Road."

Before Parker could ask him anything more, he took off running again. When he hit the sidewalk, he turned back and called out, "Hey, lady!"

Parker looked over just as the kid flipped her the bird. She didn't care, though. Her mind was on Nancy Sinclair, Hurricane Williams, and Resurrection Road.

TWENTY

BEAU JENKO WAS the first on the scene at Patrick's Garage & Gas. He had been the sheriff of Happydale for fifteen years, and before that, he had done his time in Vietnam. Like everybody else who had gone over there, he had seen some shit. Those images of pain and horror had the tendency to sneak up on him late at night when he wasn't expecting them and rob him of a night's sleep. But he had never, not in fifteen years on the job on top of the five years before that he'd spent in a war zone, had he seen the brutality that little blonde had laid out on that poor hunk of meat that was butchered out front of Patrick's Garage & Gas.

The blonde refused to say a word. She just dropped her weapons, of which she had many, put her hands behind her back to be handcuffed, and then calmly sat in the back of his prowler. She was covered in blood, and he was unprepared. He should have laid some plastic down in the back of the car, but he left the house in a hurry and didn't have any in the trunk, so he was going to have to hose it out later. The hospital tag around her wrist said her name was Parker Ames, but apart from that, she wasn't giving over any information.

Jenko was beat, and he was only at the beginning of the whole mess. He rubbed his face and glanced at his watch. It was a little after midnight, and there was a hell of a lot to do. He got on the radio, woke Deputy Morrison, and told him to pick up some coffee and get down to the station.

"Don't forget the coffee," he said again just before he ended the call.

The coffee was important. He had a one-week-old little boy at home. Cindy had just left the hospital, but she was struggling with the postnatal, so it was up to Jenko to look after the little guy while she rested up. He didn't mind. But after a week of no sleep, he was living on not much more than coffee and Mary James's strawberry pie from the diner across the road from the station.

When Jenko had arrived at Patrick's Garage & Gas, he'd looked around at the scene and tried to work out what the hell had happened. The other girl told him her name was Nancy Sinclair and that she had come from Cedar Springs, but she had the shakes and the tears, and after telling him her name, she really didn't say much more of anything. He'd sent her to the hospital with Deputy Grady and would have to collect a statement from her later on after she had seen the nurses.

So he had one hysterical teenage girl covered in blood, one blond killer also covered in blood, one dead gas station attendant, dead in his own service station, and an unknown victim hacked to pieces on the ground by the blond killer covered in blood. None of them had been particularly chatty, and that wasn't exactly a hell of a lot of leads to go on at that point.

Jenko, Grady, and Morrison represented the entire Happydale Sheriff's Department, and given the size of Happydale, they were more than enough… most of the time, that was. They also had one hospital, one ambulance, and one ambulance driver, Gordon. After Jenko made the call, Gordon came with the meat wagon, collected the corpses, and made his way back to Happydale Medical.

Not too much time later, Jenko climbed behind the wheel of his prowler, and with the bloody Parker Ames in the back seat, they hit the road. Patrick's Garage & Gas was a full fifteen minutes away from the center of Happydale, but in the middle of the night and as long as they didn't have to wait for a passing train from San Antoine, they should make it back without any trouble.

He glanced up into the rearview mirror at Parker. She was cool and calm, just staring out the window and watching Happydale roll past as if there were nothing in the world that bothered her.

That's some cold shit, Jenko thought to himself. She didn't look as though she had just hacked a man to death; she looked like she was just riding in the back of a car on her way to school, the mall, or some other place that a young woman might go. He'd only seen the aftermath of the massacre, and it took his hands a full forty-five minutes to stop shaking. He peeled his eyes off Parker and made a mental note to keep them on the road and not look back at her again.

The people of Happydale were good, hard-working Americans. They loved their football and their town fairs, and they were ready to help when anybody needed anything—like when old Marty Robbins needed a hip replacement and his insurance wouldn't pay up, the town chipped in and got old Marty Robbins his hip replacement. The town was good like that. If anybody needed anything, it stood up, and there it was. But that good side came with a healthy dose of a bad one to go along with it. Like a lot of other towns, Happydale had secrets, and it kept them well.

For instance, nobody knew that Dave Peters had gotten Jennifer Cameron pregnant in the back seat of his Cadillac shortly before they broke up in 1982. Over the next eight and a half months, she wore baggy clothes and left the house only to go to school. Everybody just thought she'd just stacked on weight, and the kids at school even started calling her Fattifer Cameron. She had plans of being the first person in her farming family to go to college and had even been accepted to Notre Dame. So a baby certainly wasn't in her plans for the immediate future.

The baby arrived at 8:34 a.m. on a Tuesday, while her parents were out working on the farm, and as far as she knew, the baby boy was 100% completely healthy. She'd already worked out a plan to leave the baby in a picnic basket on the steps of Father Harris's church and ring the bell. Father Harris was a good man, and he would know what to do. However, on that particular Tuesday, Father Harris was in Antelope Falls, visiting his sister. and didn't return to Happydale until Thursday. By that time, the baby was no more. Father Harris recognized the picnic basket from a cookout the church had three weeks before. He recognized it because it had accidently been left by Jennifer's mother, Ilse, and she'd come to retrieve it a couple of days later. It wasn't a big stretch for Father Harris to put together the basket, the baby, and the young Cameron girl's weight gain. So Father Harris gathered up the poor child and buried him in the small graveyard behind the church. He never said a word of it to anyone.

The people of Happydale never knew, but Happydale knew.

It was the same thing with Darrell Lee's wife. Sometime toward the end of 1968, or early 1969—nobody could really remember for certain—Darrell Lee and his wife, Fritzy, opened up a soda stand just a couple of doors down from the corner of Mable Avenue and Main Street. Most of their trade was done between the hours of three o'clock and seven o'clock in the evening, and they mostly served ice cream to the kids from Happydale High. They weren't living high on the hog, but they were making a living, and for Darrell, that was good enough. Although for Fritzy, good enough wasn't good enough for her. She wanted all the glamor, the money, and the life he had promised her before they were married. It wasn't that Darrell didn't try to give her those things, but he was what Fritzy's mother would call "low class," and he thought that a chicken dinner at the local diner was a class act.

A few months after opening Darrell Lee's Ice

Cream and Soda, Fritzy began referring to her husband as "the little ice cream man." It started off just between the pair of them, and even though Darrell told her he didn't like it, she continued to call him the little ice cream man. Before long, she was using the nickname in front of their friends. Well, to be frank, they were *her* friends because he wasn't allowed to have his friends over.

It was "little ice cream man this" and "little ice cream man that," and day after day, Darrell just took it… until one day when he didn't.

Everybody in town knew that Fritzy Lee was having an affair with a salesman from New York. He came to town every couple of weeks, and the two of them would hit up Sussman's Grill for a steak dinner followed by cocktails in the lobby of the Astoria Hotel, Happydale's best hotel, before retiring to a room upstairs. Darrell knew what was going on. Fritzy knew that Darrell knew, and the entire town knew everything. But being the polite folk that the residents of Happydale were, nobody ever said anything in mixed company. But everybody knew.

Come the first week of 1971, and Fritzy was nowhere to be seen. Not at the ice cream shop, not at the hair salon, and not at the Astoria Hotel. Eventually, Dottie who ran the post office asked Darrell about his wife. Darrell looked down at the ground

and said she was in New York. Everybody knew
what that meant, and nobody asked any questions
after that.

They should have, though, because Fritzy wasn't
in New York at all. She hadn't even left Happydale.
The truth was Fritzy Lee was hanging frozen in the
walk-in freezer of Darrell Lee's Ice Cream and Soda,
and that was where she had been for the past few
weeks.

"Little ice cream man…"

"Little ice cream man…"

"Little ice cream man…"

For hours, that was all he'd heard as she got
drunker and drunker. Darrell hadn't even realized
what he'd done until it was done. Next thing he
knew, Fritzy was bleeding out on the kitchen floor,
and the knife was in his hand. She didn't die straight
away. It took a good five minutes for her heart to
pump all the blood out of her body, and as he
watched her breathe her last breath, the only emotion
he felt was relief. He wrapped up her body in an old
blanket, drove her to the store at three in the morning, and put her in the walk-in freezer. Over the
course of the next few months, Darrell fed steak-
sized pieces of Fritzy to Barry Henderson's three
Dobermans on his afternoon walk. One thing was for

sure: nobody called him the little ice cream man again.

Bad things just happened in Happydale sometimes, and nobody really knew why.

In the beginning, Jenko figured whatever had happened at Patrick's Garage & Gas was just another one of those things.

TWENTY-ONE

JENKO PULLED up to the station and shut the engine down. The lights were on, and he could see Morrison making coffee through the window. The station had been state-of-the-art one hundred years ago, but since then, the paint had faded and the floorboards had warped. The roof leaked, the heat didn't work in the winter, and during the summer, it was like an oven. It was a twenty-by-twenty-feet room with a few desks, a gun cabinet, and a small cell in the corner, which was only bars drilled into the roof and the floor.

He pulled Parker out of the patrol, took her into the station and put her straight into the cell. He even shook the door just to double check that there was no way the psycho could get the hell out and cause any more havoc. He took off her cuffs and turned to

Morrison by the coffee machine. He was a good kid. Dumb as shit, but his heart was in the right place. Jenko put him on partly as a favor to Albert Morrison, the mayor of Happydale, and partly because nobody else applied for the job.

"If she moves," Jenko said, "shoot her."

Morrison looked up from the sugar he was stirring into his coffee. "I left my gun at home, boss."

Jenko cursed under his breath and shook his head. "Did you at least run her name?"

"I did." Instead of continuing, Morrison glanced over and got his first good look at Parker. The mere bloody sight of her caused him to freeze. In his twenty-six years, he had most likely never seen anything like it, and now that he had, it took him by surprise.

"Well, what's it say?" Jenko asked, breaking Morrison's concentration.

He snapped out of it. "Um…" Morrison swapped the coffee in his hands with the papers on the table. "We got three counts of assault. We got two counts of assault with a deadly weapon. We got one count of assault with a vehicle, various charges of theft, bribery, an escape from police custody, breaking and entering, and… one count of murder."

They both looked over at Parker.

She shrugged. "It wasn't me?"

"And twelve hours ago, she escaped from a mental institution," Morrison added.

"*That* may have been me," Parker said.

Jenko shook his head and poured a cup of coffee. "Jesus Christ," he mumbled. He couldn't believe this shit. "Get on the phone and put in a call to Amarillo. We're going to need a homicide detective, and I don't want her here any longer than she needs to be."

Nodding, Morrison picked up the phone, and as he was dialing, Parker leaned forward and asked, "Did you take the head?"

Jenko ignored her. "And find Patrick Dillon's ex-wife. She's living out in Knox City last I heard. Someone is going to have to come and identify the body."

"Did you take the head?" Parker asked again.

"Hey," Jenko snapped. "You keep your damn mouth shut."

"The only thing that's going to get the job done is full decapitation. Now, I'll ask you again—did you take the head?"

Jenko couldn't believe his ears. "No, you fucking psycho, I didn't take his head. The man, that poor bastard you just stabbed to death, has still got his head intact, thank you very much."

"He's no man."

"What?"

"He's a slasher," Parker said.

Jenko and Morrison swapped a very confused look.

"A slasher?" Jenko asked.

"Sometimes a man is filled with so much evil that not even hell wants him. They stay in our world. They hunt, and they kill. They're stronger than we are, and they don't feel any pain. And they don't ever, and I mean ever, give up. In short, a slasher is a real pain in the ass."

Jenko and Morrison swapped another look.

"Horseshit," Jenko said. "You're full of fucking horseshit. He's not a goddamn monster. He's just a man. Plain and goddamn simple. Like any other man out there. You know what? You can do us all a favor and not talk again, ever."

Parker sat down on the stool in the corner of her cell and shook her head. It wasn't the first time her advice had been dismissed as crazy talk. "It's all fun and games until somebody loses their head."

TWENTY-TWO

DR. JEREMIAH ELLIS spent the day searching for Parker Ames. He combed the area around the Paris, Texas, mental asylum, and after questioning the clerks of four flea-ridden motels and two gas stations, he still had no leads or clues whatsoever. At the last gas station, he bought his third coffee for the night and was sitting on the hood of his car, looking out into the quiet neon-drenched street. It had been close to twenty-four hours since she had escaped, and twenty-four hours was more than enough time to disappear within the borders of the United States or go and murder a whole lot of people.

Every hour on the hour, Ellis checked in with his answering service to see if he had any messages. Gabriele was on shift that night, and although she didn't say it, Ellis could hear in her voice that she was sick and tired of hearing from him, every hour on the hour. There was no more at stake in calling again than Gabriele's inconvenience, though, so after he finished his coffee, Ellis slid off the hood of the car, tossed his Styrofoam cup in the trash, and dropped a dime into the pay phone. It rang twice, as it always did, and when Gabriele answered, the annoyance in her voice was gone. Before he could even ask, she told him that he *did* indeed have a massage.

One. Single. Message.

He held his breath and hoped it was something that was anything. He hoped that it was Administrator Dawkins telling him they had found Parker Ames, that she hadn't hurt anybody, everything was all right, and he could go home to his Talking Heads record, his pot, and his booze.

"What's the message?" Ellis asked so quickly that all the words ran together.

"Call Sheriff Beau Jenko of Happydale, Texas. Topic, Parker Ames."

Relief and panic hit him at the same time. Ellis took down the number, dropped another coin into the slot, and punched in the number Gabriele had given him.

TWENTY-THREE

JENKO WAS HALFWAY through lighting a cigarette when the telephone rang. He scooped it up and wedged it between his ear and his shoulder as he slipped the pack of Camels back into his shirt pocket.

"Happydale Sheriff," he mumbled with the butt in in his mouth.

"This is Dr. Ellis, Sheriff. Do you have her?"

Jenko shot a glance over at Parker behind bars and sitting on a stool. "Yeah, I got her."

Parker gave him a wave.

"Is she detained?"

"She's in a cell."

"That's good… that's good," Ellis said. "Don't let her out."

"That was the plan," Jenko said as he gripped the telephone and stood up. "Look, Doc, what's the deal here? I've got one girl in the hospital and two dead bodies. What am I looking at?"

"Sheriff, Parker Ames is the most dangerous and brutal killer I've ever known."

Jenko looked at the twenty-something girl sitting across from him. "Parker Ames?"

"Yes, sir," Ellis said. "Parker Ames."

To Jenko, apart from the blood on her clothes, she looked like any other college kid. "Are we talking about the same girl?"

"She hunts what she calls 'slashers,'" Ellis said.

"She's mentioned some of those."

"In my opinion, she has one of the most severe delusional schizophrenia cases I've ever seen. According to her, slashers are, or to use better words, were men that are too evil for hell. They wander the earth, killing whoever they think has wronged them, and it's her job to…"

"To take their heads and send them back to hell," Jenko finished his words for him. "Look, Doc. Do you actually believe this shit?"

"Absolutely not," Ellis said. "It's absurd. As I said, she suffers with delusional schizophrenia. She created this world for herself. She created these… slashers."

"Why?"

"To deal with a traumatic event in her past," he

said. "Look, Sheriff. It's very important that you do not under any circumstances release her from that cell."

"I wasn't planning to," Jenko said. "But why all this anxiety if this is all in her head?"

"Sheriff," Ellis said, changing the tone in his voice to something a little more subtle, "it doesn't matter if we don't believe in slashers. Parker Ames does, and she'll stop at nothing to kill one and everything that stands in her way."

The doctor told him that he was heading to Happydale right away, but Jenko told him not to bother. Those who were dead were dead, and those who'd done the killing were behind bars. But the doctor insisted, and if the doctor wanted to waste his time, who was Jenko to argue?

TWENTY-FOUR

MEANWHILE, on the other side of town, Gordon was behind the wheel of the one and only ambulance the Happydale Medical owned. The town had a population of three thousand people, so Gordon figured, theoretically, Happydale needed an ambulance in the event that somebody was injured, was involved in a car accident, had a heart attack, or even just had a false alarm. But the reality of it was, Gordon rarely drove the vehicle, and most of the time, it stayed in the hospital emergency bay. He took it out when he picked up some of the older Happydale citizens to bring them in for their checkups or to the local school to let the little ones sit behind the wheel, but apart from that, the ambulance rarely left the hospital.

When the phone rang and Sheriff Jenko asked him to bring the ambulance out to Patrick's Garage &

Gas to pick up a couple of bodies, he didn't think twice about it. Then he arrived at the gas station and saw that one of those bodies was Patrick himself. Well, he simply couldn't keep it together. He had known Patrick Hollingsworth going on close to thirty years. They weren't terribly close, but on more than one occasion, they'd had a few beers together and shared a few laughs. Gordon always made a point to gas up the ambulance over there at the service station even though it was out of his way and the BP was closer. Patrick always got a kick out of seeing the flashing lights, and if he was honest about it, Gordon got a kick out of Patrick getting a kick out of the lights, so he always turned them on when he left. He wouldn't say they were friends, but they were certainly friendly, and seeing him like that shook Gordon up. He was certainly going to go home and drink a bottle of Wild Turkey after he got back to the hospital. That much, he had already decided.

He took a mouthful of the warm Dr Pepper that had been sitting open in the center console for the past couple of hours, wiped his mouth with the back of his hand, and looked over his shoulder at the two body bags in the back. The smaller one was Patrick. It was regular in size and shape. But the other one? He was a big boy. It had taken three of them to get him in the ambulance, and even then, it hadn't been easy.

They were all covered in sweat by the end, and Gordon was pretty sure he'd pulled a muscle in his shoulder.

Gordon yawned and wound down the window to let the warm night air flow through the car and wake him up a little. Then he kept his eyes on the dark road ahead and tried to forget about the two bodies he had in the back. What Gordon didn't know—and there really was no way that he could have known—was that while he was driving, there was movement in the back of the ambulance. The body bag containing Hurricane Williams slowly sat up straight.

There was a moment or two where Gordon just drove down the road without any idea of the horror that was about to unfold. Then for some reason, most likely out of habit, Gordon glanced in the rearview mirror. When he saw the body bag, he screamed.

The ambulance swerved violently all over the empty road and was dangerously close to crashing into the ditch, but it managed to stay on the blacktop. As soon as it straightened up, it started to lose speed and came to a complete stop by the time it reached the train crossing. The ambulance stayed quiet for a very long time. There was no movement, and the only sound was the idling engine.

Eventually, the double doors at the rear of the ambulance opened, and the colossus that was Hurricane Williams stepped out. Despite the stabbing match and the two bullets Parker had thrown his way, Hurricane moved as if nothing at all had happened to him. He stepped off and walked down the road. There was something in his hand and dangling low by his knee.

It was the head of Gordon, Happydale's only ambulance driver.

TWENTY-FIVE

HAPPYDALE MEDICAL SAT at the bottom of a dead-end street. Back in 1956, when it was built, the street was busy, with stores lining each side of the road. Over the years, though, each of those stores had closed one by one. Some blamed the economy, others blamed Happydale's diminishing population, but nobody really knew for sure. All anybody knew was that opening a store on Floyd Avenue was a surefire way to throw away a life's savings.

The hospital itself wasn't anything special, but it was all Happydale had, and it was more than they needed. The three-story building was complete with a nursery, an emergency room, a rehabilitation facility, and enough beds for fifty patients to each have their own room. The mayor who'd overseen building the hospital back in '56 had overestimated Happydale's need for it, and as a result, the hospital has never been at capacity. Over the years, as the population of the town shrank, various parts of the hospital had been shut down or closed. The rooms on the second and third floor hadn't been used in years, but nevertheless their lights were always turned on for safety. By 1988, the hospital ran on a skeleton crew.

On that night, the two nurses on shift were Irene Mandel and Jessica Hopkins. Irene was working a double and had started earlier that evening, while Jessica was on her way to start the graveyard shift. She lived a few blocks away and was listening to a mixtape on her Walkman and smoking a cigarette as she walked to work.

"You're too good for this town," her mother would always tell her, and in a way, she believed it. For as far back as she could remember, she'd dreamed about getting out of Happydale. It wasn't that she wanted to be famous or change the world. All Jessica Hopkins wanted was just simply more. More of what, she didn't really know or couldn't put her finger on it. All she knew was that Happydale wasn't going to give it to her.

Yet there she still was. Ten years after graduating high school, she had come to the realization that slowly but surely she had turned into her mother, nothing but a small-town girl. She was still dating her high school sweetheart, more out of habit than anything else, and every Friday night, she and Kevin went down to Frankie's on 5th Street to listen to the jukebox, drink beer, and talk about their high school days with the exact same friends they'd had in high school. She laughed along at their jokes and slow danced with Kevin to Springsteen, and the next Friday night, they would go down to Frankie's and do it all again.

That was until she'd found a pair of Calvin Klein underwear in the back seat of Kevin's pickup. The underwear didn't belong to her; Jessica was a Fruit of the Loom girl, not a Calvin Klein girl. She didn't know who they belonged to, and she didn't really care. That was what shocked her the most: she simply didn't care.

That had been three days ago, and in those three days, Jessica had packed a bag, which was currently slung over her shoulder, and she'd bought a ticket for the Greyhound, which was in the aforementioned bag. After she finished her shift at ten in the morning, she was going to climb aboard that bus and go to Florida. Did she know anyone in Florida? Nope? Did she have a job waiting for her in Florida? Nope. Could she start out from scratch in Florida? Absolutely. And at ten in the morning, when she stepped on board that Greyhound bus, that was exactly what she was going to do. First, though, she to finish one last shift at the hospital.

Jessica pulled off her headphones as she walked through the double doors and into the hospital lobby. As usual, it was empty, and as usual, Irene, the head nurse, was in the nurses' station with nothing but a dirty look on her face, and that dirty look was directed Jessica's way.

"You're late," the old battle-ax said.

"It's not like we have any patients anyway."

"We have one tonight," Irene said.

Jessica stopped dead in her tracks. They hadn't had a patient in two weeks, and that was when the Glover kid had an asthma attack.

"She's in Room Four," Irene said.

Jessica quickly headed to the change room and slipped into her scrubs, then she made her way down the empty corridor to Room 4. When she walked inside and saw Nancy Sinclair, Jessica paused at the sight of her. The poor girl looked as if she had been through hell. Her clothes were torn and frayed. Her hair a mess, and various cuts and bruises covered her skin. It was the fear in her face that struck Jessica more than anything else, though.

She gave Nancy the same spiel she'd given every patient she had ever seen. She told her that she was going to be all right. That she was there to help fix her up. And that nothing bad was going to happen to them. Those words weren't always true, but ninety-nine percent of the patients believed her, and they felt just a little bit better. When she said those words to Nancy Sinclair, the girl gave her half a glance, and Jessica knew that Nancy Sinclair fell into that other one percent.

Most of the blood wasn't hers. The girl was covered in superficial cuts and bruises but nothing major or anything that would cause long-term damage. In a few weeks, all her injuries would heal, and within a year, any scars would most likely fade.

'So, what happened here?" Jessica asked as she put the final dressing on a graze on Nancy's knee.

"Bad luck."

"Do you know what my grammy used to say about bad luck?" Jessica asked.

"No. I don't know what your grammy used to say about bad luck."

"She used to say that you never know what worse luck your bad luck just saved you from."

Nancy raised an eyebrow. She totally wasn't in the mood, and Jessica got the message.

She finished up the dressing and rose to her feet. "You've got some cuts and bruises, nothing that won't heal over time. All in all, I'd say you're going to live."

"Lucky for me," Nancy said. "Is there a phone here?"

There was one on the wall, and Jessica told her that all she had to do was dial zero to get an outside line.

Some patients needed hugs. Some patients just needed to be left alone. Nancy Sinclair was one of the ones who needed to be left alone.

TWENTY-SIX

NANCY WAITED until the nurse was out of the room before she dialed the number to her house. She meant to be at Heather's hours ago, and no doubt Heather would have called her house when Nancy didn't arrive. Her mom must have been worried sick. She never did well in times of high stress, so Nancy wasn't going to tell her an ax murderer had tried to kill her on Resurrection Road. She would tell her mom that the car broke down, and she would be home in a few hours. Nancy figured it would be best to wait until they were face-to-face to come clean about the whole bloody affair.

They had spent the past week fighting, and what they were fighting over, Nancy couldn't even remember. It might've started when her mother said she couldn't go to Jenny Ascot's party in Valpo, but

Nancy had gone anyway, which only made things worse. Then every little thing they could possibly disagree over, they found a way to disagree. Thinking back, it wasn't even the last couple of weeks. It was more like the past couple of years had been filled with disagreements, fights, and snark. They had been fighting for so long that it was just the way it was, and Nancy she couldn't think of any reason why. It was just the way things were.

For as far back as she could remember, every single year on her mother's birthday, the pair of them would get dressed up and travel into Dallas, where they would have tea at the world-famous Devonshire Tea House. Nancy didn't know if the Devonshire Tea House was indeed world-famous or how Devonshire tea was different from regular tea, but it was a tradition. Every single year.

Every single year except for that year because on her mom's birthday, which had been just a few days ago, Nancy was grounded for sneaking out to that party. She was granted a day pass for the tea house tradition, but Nancy had stayed home. Nancy could say that rules were rules, that being grounded meant being grounded, but at the end of the day, the real reason Nancy didn't go to Dallas was that she was simply being a bitch. She stayed in her room while her mother got all dressed up, she stayed in her room while her mother asked her if she wanted to go, and she stayed in her room when she heard her mother crying from down the hall.

Nancy wished she could take it all back—every single last bitchy word. She wished she could get into a time machine, get all dressed up, and take her mom out to tea in Dallas for her birthday. She may have missed her mom's last birthday, but from that day forward Nancy made a pact with herself that she would never miss another.

She pushed the digits on the phone then listened to the dial tone as she waited for somebody to pick up on the other end. She waited.

And waited.

And waited.

The answering machine kicked in.

"Hello, you've reached, Wayne, Liz, and Nancy Sinclair. We're all busy and can't get to the phone right now. So leave a message, and one of us will get back to you."

"Mom… if you're there, pick up…" Nancy let out a long, it's-been-an-exhausting-night kind of sigh. "I just wanted to say I love you and I'll be home soon."

She hung up, dialed again, and listened to the phone ring again. Then she listened to the answering machine message again.

"Mom, if you're there, please pick up." Nancy

waited for someone to come on the line, but nobody did.

She called again and listened to the message again. When nobody answered, she hung up and repeated the process. No matter how many times she rang, nobody was answering that phone.

What Nancy didn't know, and there was no possible way she could have known, was that over at 25 Chatsworth Road in Cedar Springs, Wayne and Liz had been paid a visit by Hurricane Williams. No matter how many times she rung, nobody was answering that phone.

TWENTY-SEVEN

DEPUTY GRADY HAD JUST DROPPED off Nancy Sinclair at the hospital, and Jenko wanted him to head back to Patrick's Garage & Gas to secure the crime scene for when the homicide cops turned up from Amarillo. It was a glorified security guard job, but an order was an order.

Grady was halfway back to the filling station when a pair of red taillights emerged from the darkness. As he drove closer, he peered forward and saw the ambulance stopped in the middle of the road by the railway crossing.

Grady eased off the gas and brought the patrol car to a stop with its headlights shining on the ambulance. The rear doors were open, but apart from that, Grady really couldn't make out much more from inside the car. Given everything that had happened, Grady wasn't taking any chances, and when he climbed out of the patrol he had his 9 mm in the palm of his hand.

He looked up and down the road and didn't see another car or soul in sight. There was silence in the air, and every step he took toward the ambulance sounded like it would be heard for miles around. Very, very carefully, he approached the rear of the ambulance. With a shaky left hand, Grady unclipped the flashlight from his belt, flicked the switch, and shined it into the back of the ambulance.

What he saw inside made him throw up in his mouth. He pushed it back down but couldn't keep it down, and with his body bent over, Grady vomited every single last thing from the depths of his belly. When he was finished, he finally worked up the courage to shine a light into the back of the ambulance one last time.

Gordon had been torn to pieces, ripped apart, chewed, and destroyed.

Hurricane was nowhere in sight, and neither, as far as Grady could tell, was Gordon's head. He instantly felt unsafe and took a couple of steps away from the ambulance. He didn't know why; he just felt better about things standing out in the open, where he could see something come at him and nobody could sneak up.

Grady holstered the 9 mm, unclipped the radio from his belt, and pushed it to his lips. "Boss, it's Grady," he said. "We've got ourselves one hell of a problem."

TWENTY-EIGHT

BACK AT THE STATION, Jenko heard the radio crackle alive, so he finished the last mouthful of the third cup of coffee, cut across the station, and picked up the blower. "Jenko here."

"He's gone, boss," Grady said.

"Who's gone?"

"The victim."

"Patrick?"

"The other one."

"What do you mean 'he's gone'?"

"He's just not here anymore," Jenko said.

"Then where is he?"

"I'm not entirely sure, boss."

"What does Gordon say?"

Grady looked down at the headless corpse of the

ambulance diver. "I'm not sure he has a hell of a lot to say. He's dead."

"Goddamn it!" Jenko snapped.

From back over by the cell, Parker watched and listened to everything.

"Just get back here as soon as you can," Jenko said as he put the radio down.

Parker watched as Jenko paced the room. He took a couple of steps in one direction, ran his fingers through his greasy hair, and took a couple of steps in the other direction. "He's coming for you," she said. "He's coming for all of us."

"Ah, horseshit," Jenko snapped. "Nobody's coming."

Then out of nowhere, something flew through the window, sending glass all over the place and scaring the shit out of everybody. It hit the ground and rolled across the floor.

Parker cocked her head and got a better angle. Sitting up against the floor and the bottom of a desk was the severed head of the ambulance driver, Gordon.

"I guess somebody's here," Parker said.

"Jesus Christ," Jenko said as his gaze shifted from the severed head to the window it had just smashed through. He saw something out there and took a couple of steps closer to get a better look. When he was at the window frame, Morrison joined him, and they both peered into the darkness. Standing out on the middle of the road was the gigantic Hurricane Williams.

"We are so fucked," Morrison said.

Jenko pulled his revolver, opened the cylinder, and checked the rounds. His gun was fully loaded. "Calm down. I bet you're regretting leaving your weapon at home now."

"Mom said regrets aren't good for anyone," Morrison said.

"Your mom may be wrong about this one." Hanging off the coat stand by the front door was an old school baton. Jenko pulled it down and held it out for Morrison. "You're going to have to make do with this."

Morrison held it in his hand. "What's the plan?"

Jenko looked out the window again at Hurricane. "We're gonna ask him politely to come inside and have a little chat."

"And if he doesn't want to come in?" Morrison asked.

"We might have to ask him not so politely." Jenko drew in a deep breath. This was not something he was terribly keen on doing in a hurry. "You ready?"

"No," Morrison said.

"We have to go out there," Jenko said. "We can't not."

Morrison nodded. "Let's get this over and done with."

They both stepped toward the door, and just as they were almost out, Parker called out to them, "Hey."

Jenko stopped and looked over his shoulder.

"Let me out," she said. "I'll fight with you."

"The last thing I need is two psychos on the loose," Jenko said.

And with that, the two Happydale cops walked out into the night. Parker couldn't see much from inside the cell, but she could hear every single word, and based on what she was listening to, Parker was pretty sure things were probably not going in favor of the Happydale Sheriff's Department.

"Hey, buddy," Jenko said. "My colleague and I here would appreciate it if you would do us a favor and drop that great big damned knife you're holding there."

Silence…

"In case I wasn't clear the first time," Jenko continued. "Drop the damn knife."

More silence…

"Buddy, if you don't put that knife down and comply with what I'm telling you, we will be forced to use a higher degree of force, if you know what I'm saying."

Parker's fingers tightened around the bars. She had been around slashers long enough to know that precise moment, that *very* precise moment when it all goes to hell and somebody loses their life. This was shaping up to be one of those very moments.

"Have it your way," Jenko said.

And then it all went to hell.

"Boss," Morrison yelled. "Watch out! Watch out! Watch out!"

Gunfire. Three quick shots. *Bang! Bang! Bang!*

Footsteps, hard and fast.

"Boss!"

Sounds of a scuffle. Meat slapping on meat. A pounding.

Someone screamed. Not a regular scream. It was a gut-wrenching scream of fear and pain.

Parker shook the bars—no good.

Another scream.

She held her breath and listened, but all she could hear was silence, and that silence went on for what felt like forever. Not being able to see anything meant her imagination ran wild with all the horrendous violence Hurricane was doing to Jenko and Morrison. She shook the bars again, but there wasn't a chance in hell she was getting through those bastards.

Then she heard footsteps. They were coming from outside and coming on into the station. They were long, slow footsteps… and they were getting closer. When they were just on the other side of the front door, that door creaked open.

It wasn't Hurricane or Jenko; it was Morrison. He was as white as a ghost. He took one shuffling step, followed by another shuffling step, then another after that. He moved as if motion sent shockwaves of pain throughout his entire body, and he was just trying to push the pain out of his mind and keep moving forward. The baton dropped from his fingers and hit the floorboards with a clunk.

"You're not looking too good there, buddy," Parker said.

Blood rolled out of his eyes like tears and ran down his cheeks.

He fell to his knees. Despair replaced the fear on his face as if he'd just come to terms with his fate and his whole life had been one long regret. Then he fell face-first onto the floor, and in that moment, Parker saw Hurricane's great big, bloody machete buried halfway into the back of Morrison's skull.

For a moment, Parker had thought that maybe Morrison had a chance of surviving this mess. But nobody survived a machete to the back of the skull. It didn't matter how optimistic they were.

Parker heard more footsteps… big, heavy… and coming right in the front door. Of course, it was the big, bad Hurricane that walked on in as if he owned the joint. He paused over Morrison's corpse and wrapped his fingers around the machete. And when he pulled it out, a spray of blood flew across the station and splattered across the desks. Hurricane turned his head Parker's way.

She gave a shy wave. "This is awkward."

Blade in hand, he rushed toward her. There were only a few steps to the cell on the other side of the station, and Hurricane wasted no time in getting there. He swung his shoulder back and thrusted the blade between the cell bars at her.

Parker jumped. She hit the wall and pushed herself as far back into it as she possibly could. Hurricane swiped, and slashed, and stabbed, but he was just out of range. With the blade inches away from cutting her up, she couldn't move. Not one single centimeter. If she tilted even ever so slightly, she would be cut to ribbons. So she just stayed there, with her back to the wall, not moving a muscle, as the blade slashed past her face.

Hurricane must have realized he was wasting his time and slowed his slashing and swiping and pulled his arm back through the bars and out of the cell altogether.

Parker smiled, feeling cocky. "Not so much of a smarty-pants now, are you?"

Hurricane stared her down for a moment, and she knew—man, she knew—he was calculating something inside that masked head of his. Then Hurricane took a couple of steps back over to Morrison's body and unclipped a set of keys from his belt. They were the keys to the station—keys to the cell.

"Uh-oh," Parker said. "This isn't going to be good."

Hurricane moved closer with the key in his hand and aimed right for the lock. Naturally, Parker was starting to panic. There weren't exactly a hell of a lot of options for a woman in her position.

The key hit the lock. Groove by groove, it slid all the way in, and before he turned the key and opened the door, he paused. She could see his bloodshot eyes peer out through the holes in his mask. They were face-to-face, one inside the cage and the other outside.

Parker had one move left. She put her hand between two of the bars, and with her palm, she slammed Hurricane's fist, breaking the key in the lock. She was well and truly trapped in there now.

Hurricane looked down at the lock then back up at Parker. Although he didn't actually say a word, Parker could tell by the look in his eyes that if he'd been the talking kind, the word that would have leaked out of his lips would have been *bitch*.

Hurricane could kick down doors. He could punch a car to death. He could get stabbed, shot, and hung then still come back to life. What he couldn't do, though—and Parker knew this from experience—was break out of a cell. By that logic, there was a very high chance that he couldn't break into one either. He came to the same conclusion pretty quickly, then slowly, he turned around and with the same considered steps that he'd walked into the station with, he walked back out.

Even slashers had their limitations.

Parker may have survived the attack, but the harsh reality of the situation was that she was still stuck in a cell, and everyone with a key had just very recently been hacked to pieces.

She called out a hello, but the only thing that came back at her was a big fat silence.

She slumped down on the bench. "This is turning out to be one hell of a long and shitty night." He didn't say it. In fact, Hurricane Williams didn't say much, but he didn't need to. Parker knew he was headed to the hospital and straight to Nancy Sinclair, and unless she got out of that goddamned cell, Hurricane would find Nancy and separate one, if not more, of Nancy's limbs from her body and do the same to anybody else who stood in his way.

Parker rattled the door for the millionth time, and the result was the same—locked. She pushed her face between the bars and sighed. "It's times like these where you start second-guessing some of your life choices."

Then something grabbed her attention. On one of the desks, all wrapped up in little evidence bags, were an assortment of Parker's weapons. Her .45 and the bloodstained machete from Patrick's Garage & Gas were there, but on top of that, Jenko must have searched her car and pulled out all the other weapons she'd collected from the cemetery. There they sat, out on display for all to see.

Parker's eyes settled on her chain saw, Aerosmith. "Hello, old friend."

The desk wasn't close, but it was the closest desk to the cell, and maybe, just maybe, she could reach it.

Parker pushed her arm out between two bars, stretched her fingers out, and jammed her shoulder between two bars to reach the desk. The combination of all those things seemed to help, and the very tips of Parker's fingers touched, just *barely* touched, Aerosmith's handle. Her index finger hooked around the handle loop.

Parker smiled to herself, because if anything was

better than having the key to the cell you were trapped in, it was having a chain saw. She was almost home free when her finger slipped and the chain saw fell to the floor… way, way out of reach.

Parker let out a long sigh that deflated almost all of her as she looked at the chain saw. "That totally sucks."

TWENTY-NINE

GRADY WAS STILL SHAKEN up after seeing Gordon's body in the back of the ambulance. After he got off the radio with Jenko, he sat in his car for close to twenty minutes, just staring straight ahead. He had never seen anything like that in his life. Sure, he had seen a hundred horror movies at the Nazareth drive-in when he was in high school, but not one of them were anything like what he had seen in the back of the Happydale ambulance. He couldn't sit there all night—he knew that much—so Grady picked up the radio and put it to his lips. He tried to raise Jenko and Morrison, but neither of them responded. He wasn't being much good to anyone sitting in his car, so he climbed out and very tentatively, with very tiny baby steps, made his way to the rear of the ambulance. Looking straight up at the sky, he closed the rear doors. Then he locked the ambulance and took the keys, figuring he would go back to the station and get orders from Jenko. All the while, the ambulance would be locked and safe. If someone did stumble across it—which was most likely a long shot, given it was the middle of the night—they would just drive on past, oblivious to the horror inside.

Back in the patrol car, he wound the windows down and let the night air wash the horror off him. Grady didn't drink or smoke, but driving back to the station, he felt like doing both.

Happydale was quiet. There were no cars on the road, not that there would have been at that time anyway, and the houses he passed were all quiet and dark. There wasn't even the blue glow of a late-night television leaking out through the gaps in the curtains of any of the houses.

Grady pulled the car to the side of the road in front of the station, and he knew instantly something was wrong. At first, he couldn't quite put his finger on it and figured that maybe he was still jumpy, but as soon as the headlights of his patrol car flashed the front of the station, casting a sheen over the fresh blood on the concrete, he knew his nerves had every right to be on edge. A flashlight lay on the sidewalk, shining a light on nothing in particular, and the door to the station was wide open.

That door was never wide open.

He palmed his revolver from the holster on his hip and slowly made his way across the sidewalk and up the path to the station. Even with his ears and eyes peeled for any bump in the night and his heart pounding, Grady was still careful not to step in any of the blood on the concrete as he made his way up to the door.

The lights were on, and the first thing he saw was Morrison facedown in a pool of his own blood. Grady dropped a knee and slipped two fingers on Morrison's neck to check for a pulse, but after a couple of seconds of waiting and hoping, there was no pulse whatsoever.

"Dang," Grady muttered as he leaned back on his heels, trying to make sense of the whole situation. It took a couple of moments, but the cop in him kicked in, and when he opened his eyes, Grady knew he had to get a handle on this situation.

Grady scanned the room. Except for the psycho in the cage, the station was empty. His eyes locked onto Parker behind the bars. "What happened?"

"He tripped and fell," she said.

"Really?"

"What? No!" Parker said. "What do you think happened?"

Grady used the table to climb to his feet. "Where's Jenko?"

"He went outside with him," she said, motioning to Morrison's corpse. "He didn't come back, so it's probably safe to assume that he didn't make it. Hurricane Williams is headed to the hospital. We need to get there, A-SAP."

Grady dragged his eyes away from his friend's body to the psycho in the cage. "Why?"

"To finish what he started," Parker said. "Find a key and get me the hell out of here."

Grady wasn't so sure.

"How do I know you're not the killer?" Grady asked. "How do I know you didn't do this to Morrison, huh?"

"Why would I kill him and get back in the cell? If I wanted to escape, it defeats the purpose of having killed him in the first place," Parker said.

That made sense—at least to Grady at the time.

"You can't do this yourself," she said.

He knew that was true. "But no weapons," Grady said as he dug his hand into the pocket of his pants for the cell keys.

"Not even a small one?" Parker asked.

"Nope. Not even a small one."

THIRTY

JESSICA HOPKINS WAS AT THE NURSES' station when she saw a dark figure standing in the parking lot. She had spent the better part of the night with her chin in her palm, leaning on the desk and just staring at the clock. There were only three hours until her shift was over. Only three hours until she left Kevin, Happydale, and her whole shitty life behind. But if she kept staring at the clock like she had for the past two hours, those three hours were going to take a lifetime to pass.

And then there was that dark figure standing out there in the parking lot. Jessica had no idea how long he had been standing there, and after watching him for a couple of seconds, it didn't seem like he was moving or doing anything other than standing in the empty parking lot and staring at the hospital. Jessica had seen a lot of scary stuff at Happydale Medical, or her imagination ran wild and tricked her into thinking she had seen a lot of scary stuff. There was that time in her first week when she'd thought she saw the body bag containing old Jeffrey Shaw move in the morgue. Or the time she'd thought the entire second floor was haunted—to be fair, she *had* just watched *Poltergeist* and thought everything was haunted at the time. Naturally, an empty hospital was a scary place, but after three years, Jessica was used to all the crazy, scary scenarios that her mind cooked up. Very little bothered her anymore, even the things that should scare her—like a dark figure standing in the parking lot alone. Any reasonable person would have locked the doors, called the police, and hidden. Jessica wasn't so easily scared anymore, though.

Jessica called out for Irene, but she was sneaking a cigarette on the east side of the building. Eleven months ago, Irene had told her husband and everybody else that she'd quit, but she'd never fully shaken the habit. Even though Jessica never let on, she could always smell the Camels on her.

"Hey, Irene," she called out again but didn't get any response.

Jessica sighed and climbed to her feet. She figured she'd better go out there and see what was going on.

Whoever it was could be lost, drunk, or legitimately sick. They were still a hospital after all, even considering the serious lack of patients.

She pushed through the double doors and wrapped her arms around her middle to keep warm. "Hello," she called out. "Is everything okay?"

The figure didn't call back; he didn't even budge. He just stood there like a statue.

"Hellooo?" Jessica called out again.

There was a light fog in the air. Not a lot, just enough to make Jessica squint a little to see his face. She was still too far, and it was still too dark to make out any sort of detail, though. She looked back over her shoulder to see if Irene was back from her smoke break, but all she saw was the empty nurses' station.

"Shit," she muttered to herself, but she didn't start to get worried until she looked back in the direction of the figure and saw he was gone. "That's probably not a good thing."

Jessica turned on her heels and headed back to the hospital. She threw a glance back over her shoulder and saw nothing but darkness and fog. She must've wandered thirty or forty feet through the parking lot and was starting to feel that the gap between her and the safe confines of the hospital was too great. Her walk turned into a jog, and a couple of steps after that, her jog turned into a run.

She heard footsteps behind her, and they were running just as fast as she was. Jessica pumped her arms and pounded her feet on the concrete. She was just at the double doors to the entrance to the hospital when she felt fingers wrap around her arm. They dragged her to a stop. Jessica didn't skip a beat. There's no way in hell she was going to let anything happen to her just so close to getting the hell out of this shithole town, so she clenched her fist, turned, and swung.

She hit him square in the face and heard the slap of flesh on flesh, then she threw her hands up to her mouth when she realized what she had done. The figure in the parking lot wasn't a crazed lunatic or a demented killer; he was no one more than her piece-of-shit boyfriend, Kevin.

"What the hell, Kevin!" Jessica yelled.

He was still half bent over, recovering from the blow. "Wow, what was that for?"

"Well…" She tried to find the words to explain. "I thought you were…"

"You thought I was what?"

"I don't know," she said. "One minute, you were there. The other, you weren't. What were you doing chasing me?"

"I wasn't chasing you? You were running, and I

was running after you." Kevin finally stood upright, rubbing his jaw.

"Are you okay?" Jessica asked.

"Sure, I guess," he said. "Lucky you hit like a girl."

And it was that line that reminded Jessica why she was leaving Kevin and that entire small-thinking town.

"What are you doing here, Kevin?" Her tone had shifted from concerned to annoyed.

"I was just down at Frankie's with Roy and Dinger…"

That was bullshit. Jessica knew he'd been with *her*. Before leaving the house, he'd put on his Ralph Lauren underwear that she had bought him for Christmas and slapped on more than a healthy dose of Brut, which he still reeked of.

"… and I bumped into Laney. You remember Laney from school?"

She remembered Laney from school. "Yeah, so what?"

"Well, the interesting thing is that Laney now works down at the bus depot, and according to Laney, she said she saw you buy a one-way ticket to Florida earlier today."

"Maybe Laney was mistaken."

"That crossed my mind as well," Kevin said. "Then do you know what I did?"

Jessica crossed her arms. "No, Kevin. What did you do?"

"I went home and checked the closet." He started counting off on his fingers. "Your bag was gone, half your clothes, and that ugly teddy bear that sits on the bed that you had since you were a kid. Gone, all of it."

"Maybe you didn't look well enough."

"Oh, I looked," he said.

"So what? What do you want me to say?"

"I want you to tell me the truth."

"I brought a ticket to Florida on the seven a.m. Greyhound, and I'm not coming back."

Even though he already knew everything she had just said, she knew hearing the words come out of her mouth hurt him. She didn't even warm them up. They were delivered cold and hard.

"Were you even going to tell me?" The hurt in his voice was real. He wasn't putting it on to make her feel guilty or anything.

"No," she said. "I wasn't."

"This is a joke, yeah?"

She shook her head. "No, Kevin. This is not a joke."

"I don't get it. I fucking love you, Jessica. I fucking love you. I was going to propose to you."

"What?" She laughed. "When?"

"Next week at the drive-in."

"At the drive-in?"

"Yes. *The Lost Boys* is playing."

"Are you nuts?"

"You love Corey Haim."

"That doesn't mean I want to get engaged while watching a Corey Haim movie," she said. "Why don't you propose to Molly Henderson during *The Lost Boys*?"

"What's that supposed to mean?"

"You know what it means," Jessica said as she took one last look at the boy she had just wasted the last ten years of her life with, then she turned around and headed back for the hospital doors.

"I will marry you, Jessica Hopkins. You're my girl," he shouted. "You mark my words. We will be—"

The door closed behind her as Jessica stepped back into the hospital, and when the door closed behind her, Jessica couldn't hear another word from Kevin.

The truth was she'd been scared to tell him she was leaving. That was why she simply hadn't. It was easier to buy a ticket, pack a few things, and just disappear. She wasn't afraid he would hit her or anything like that. She was afraid that she wouldn't be able to go through with it if she told him to his face, then she would never leave. As it turned out, telling him in person was a lot easier than she'd thought.

She didn't even look back over her shoulder to have one last look at the boy she used to love. That was probably a good thing, because if she had, she would have seen not only Kevin standing in the empty parking lot, but also Hurricane Williams towering right behind him.

Kevin, the poor son of a bitch, had no idea the slasher was there until Hurricane's dinner-plate-sized hands clamped onto Kevin's skull and squeezed. His fingers broke the skin, and within seconds, they were crushing Kevin's skull. Before long, his head was nothing but mush, and Kevin was nothing more than another piece of collateral damage on Hurricane's bloody rampage.

THIRTY-ONE

THEY TOLD her to get some rest, to just lay in bed, close her eyes, and fall asleep—but Nancy tried all that. And she still couldn't sleep. In theory, it sounded like sound advice after she'd escaped a crazed lunatic, but no matter how hard she tried, Nancy just couldn't get to sleep. She tossed and turned, and she watched MTV. But after a couple of hours of that, she was still wide awake.

Enough is enough, Nancy thought. Beside the cuts and the bruises, she felt one hundred percent healthy, and those cuts and bruises weren't anything that that couldn't be solved with a Diet Pepsi and a nice long bath.

She swung her feet over the edge of the bed, slipped them into the hospital slippers on the floor, and made her way over to the closet in the corner of the room. Deputy Grady had taken her clothes. "They're evidence," he'd said as he bagged them up just before he left. He was going to come straight back with fresh clothes from his little sister, who was around her same age and height, but when he didn't come back, the nurses raided the lost and found and came up with a pair of Levi's shorts and an Esprit tee. The only shoes they had were one size-twelve Reebok and one size-ten Converse. They'd be more trouble than they were worth, so Nancy opted to go barefoot since she figured her mother was going to pick her up anyway.

She had tried to call her mom a couple of times in the last few hours, but she couldn't get through. *Dad must have turned the ringer down again,* she thought. He always said it was up too loud, and when it rang, it would make him almost jump out of his skin. Nancy figured he had turned it down before they went to sleep and forgotten to turn it back up.

Nancy pulled off the hospital gown and slid into the shorts and shirt. It crossed her mind to head straight down to the nurses' station, but she figured they would make her stay. So she wrote a note that said that she was all okay and feeling tons better then left it on the bed. She would call the Happydale Sheriff's Department in the morning to make a statement or give an interview or whatever they needed her to do, but in the meantime, she'd had enough of this joint, and she was out of there.

Very quietly, Nancy made her way down to the first-floor emergency room where Jessica had patched up her knee. She heard voices coming from the nurses' station and figured the coast was clear. Just in case, Nancy opened the door a crack and peeked through.

The coast certainly was clear. She carefully closed the door behind her, wedged the phone between her ear and neck, and dialed her best friend's phone number.

THIRTY-TWO

BEST FRIENDS FOREVER. That was what Heather and Nancy had decided they would be when they were six-years-old, and from that moment on, that was exactly what they were. Every Saturday night since they were twelve years old, either Heather would stay at Nancy's house or Nancy would stay at Heather's house. Sometimes, they would paint their nails. Sometimes, they would bake cupcakes, but mostly, though, they would talk about boys and watch movies. That particular Saturday night, Nancy had intended to drive over to Heather's, and they were going to watch *The Legend of Billie Jean* for like the one hundredth time. That had been the plan anyway, but Nancy never showed, which was very un-Nancy like. After half an hour, Heather thought it was unusual. After an hour, she started to worry.

After an hour and fifteen minutes, she called Nancy's house, but no one answered. For the rest of the night, Heather sat right next to the Garfield phone by the side of her bed and just stared at it, willing it to ring with nothing but the power of her mind. Of course, it would be Nancy on the other end of the line with some story about why she was running late. Then she would be there in a couple of minutes, and they would have a big laugh over it all. But it was just after two o'clock in the morning, and as much as Heather wanted that to happen, deep down, she knew something was wrong.

She was lying on her bed, flicking through channels and listening to her stomach rumble—she and Nancy were on a crash diet—when the phone did actually ring in real life.

She pounced on it. "Hello," she said before the phone was even close to her lips.

Nancy was on the other line. She was at the Happydale hospital and needed a lift. Heather didn't ask why or what happened or anything like that. All she said was that she would be there in fifteen minutes and hung up.

Heather's parents were asleep, and there was no way they would let her take the car well after curfew anyway, so she sneaked down the stairs and into the kitchen. She slipped the keys off the hook by the back door and crept out into the driveway. It wasn't the first time Heather had done this. She knew from experience that her parents asleep upstairs would most likely hear the engine of their station wagon start up, so she took the hand brake off, slipped it into neutral, and rolled it down the driveway and out into the street. If she started the engine from the street, there was a pretty fair chance that no one in the Ross household would hear a thing or be none the wiser.

She turned the engine over, slipped the wagon into first, and slowly, as if that were somehow quieter, cruised down the street. She didn't even switch the radio on until she was a block away, but when she did, "Drive" by the Cars drifted out of the speakers. Heather found the song quite fitting.

Ever since third grade, when Miss Marshall introduced Nancy to the class as the new girl from Indiana, Heather had just known they were going to be friends. She didn't remember how it had happened; she just remembered that it was always Nancy and Heather. But Nancy was always first. She was the first to need a bra. She was the first of them to get her period and the first to kiss a boy. Heather would never admit it, and Nancy would never say it, but Nancy was the pretty one. Heather wasn't hideous by any stretch of the imagination—she was just average. Not tall or short. Not fat or skinny. Just average. She had average hair, average boobs, and an average smile. On a scale of one to ten, most people would say that Heather's personality was a five, or possibly even a six, depending on who was asked.

Nancy, on the other hand, was perfect. She was Heather's perfect friend. "Why can't you be more pretty like Nancy?" Heather's senile old grandmother would often ask. Heather would laugh it off, and her mother would say not to pay attention to her grandmother because she was old and didn't know what she was saying. Deep down, though, Heather knew her grandmother was right. It had been that way since they were little, and she was just used to it… or she *had been* used to it anyway. That was up until three months ago, when they were at a party at Brett Hill's house.

The South Plains had beat Silvertown fifty-six to fifty-four, and that night was the night Heather Ross was going to make out with Rick Gale. She had been drooling over him since he transferred from Wichita Falls, and she knew he was going to Brett's party because Sally Perkins sat next to him in Chem, and he'd told her so. Heather and Nancy spent all that afternoon choosing the perfect outfit. They settled on a denim skirt, which her dad said was way too short, and Nancy let Heather borrow her new vest, which she had covered with buttons and pins. She hair sprayed her hair Madonna style, put on her face, and looked at herself in the mirror. For the first time in her life, Heather looked... hot.

They arrived at the party a fashionable sixty minutes late, and the plan, which they concocted that afternoon, was to make Rick Gale come to her. She would talk to everyone but him. She would laugh and joke, and occasionally, very occasionally, she was to make eye contact with Rick, but only for a second. She didn't want to look desperate.

Everything was going according to plan. Heather's hair looked just like Madonna's in *Who's That Girl*. She was working the room and even occasionally made eye contact with Rick, but only for a couple of seconds before looking away, just like they had planned. What they hadn't planned on was Heather's nerves. Her stomach was full of butterflies, and she felt like everybody was watching her. She knew they weren't, of course, but she still felt as though they were. Consequently, she wasn't paying attention to how many coolers she was drinking. All that she knew was that she always had one in her hand, and after an hour and a half, she suddenly felt sick and ran to the bathroom. It was awful. The smell. The sound. The embarrassment.

Nancy was there, holding her hair back while

only God knew how many coolers violently blasted out of her. When it was over, she slumped between the toilet and the basin and cried. Nancy wanted to take her home, but Heather didn't want to ruin her night as well, so she made Nancy go back out to the party while she went to Brett Hill's little brother's room and lay down on his bed. Despite throwing up, her head was still spinning, and all she wanted to do was lie down and go to sleep, and that was just what she did.

Heather wasn't sure how long she had been asleep, but when she woke, the party sounded like it was winding down, with fewer voices bouncing off the walls and the music lower and smoother. She didn't feel sick anymore. She just felt like going home, having a shower and a piece of toast, and going to bed.

The living room was dark. People sat around quietly chatting and smoking cigarettes while Devon and Rob played Atari on the television. "Do You Really Want to Hurt Me," played through the speakers as she scanned the smoke and darkness, looking for Nancy. At first, she couldn't see her, but on a second glance, she found her friend on the couch, making out with a boy. That boy was Rick Gale. *Her* Rick Gale.

She felt ten times worse than what she had after

drinking all those coolers. She felt like she had been hit in the stomach and the heart at the same time and by her best friend. She didn't yell. She didn't scream. She didn't say a word. She just looked down at the floor, made her way back to Brett Hill's little brother's room, and waited for Nancy to come and wake her up.

Heather pretended to be asleep when Nancy came, and on the drive home, she never mentioned what she had seen. But she didn't forget.

THIRTY-THREE

NANCY TOLD Heather to pick her up from the rear parking lot, the one near the old Dunkin' Donuts. Not the main parking lot where the nurses in the nurses' station could see everyone who rolled up and not the staff parking lot on the east side of the hospital, but the rear parking lot. She figured that both Jessica and Irene wouldn't even think to look back there since that end of the hospital was dark and shut down.

Heather had said fifteen minutes, and Nancy knew that she would leave straight away, so if Heather said she would be there in fifteen minutes, Nancy was pretty certain that in fifteen minutes, Heather would be at the rear of the hospital and ready to go.

She's a good friend, Nancy thought. *Too good for me, anyway.*

For weeks she had been riddled with guilt. Every time she looked at Heather or heard her voice on the telephone, she felt bad about what had happened with Rick Gale. She hadn't meant for it to happen; it just kind of had. It was a mistake, and she wished she had never kissed him. To make matters worse, he wouldn't stop calling her.

Nancy had tried telling Heather, but every time she started, she would chicken out and change the subject. But not now. After tonight and everything she had gone through, she had come to the conclusion that life was too short for secrets and lies. Heather was her best friend, and best friends didn't kiss each other's crushes.

Nancy closed the door just as quietly as she'd opened it and tiptoed down the hall. She could hear the nurses chatting and figured once she was a good twenty or thirty feet down the corridor, she would be home free.

That's what she thought, anyway. What Nancy didn't know was that behind her, all the way down the other end of the hall, was Hurricane Williams.

He kept pace with Nancy. He didn't speed up his pace to get closer nor did he slow down so that the gap between them could grew. He just kept a nice measured pace as they moved through the halls of the hospital.

Nancy didn't know what it was. She couldn't quite put her finger on it, but she knew that something wasn't right. Maybe it was the scary-as-hell empty hospital. Maybe it was the psycho who'd attacked her at Patrick's Garage & Gas, or maybe it was the combination of the two, but Nancy knew something was fishy. All of a sudden, she felt vulnerable as she walked down the empty hall.

She slowed her steps and came to a stop. Behind her, Hurricane did the same. Slowly, very slowly, she looked over her shoulder and saw the hulking silhouette of Hurricane Williams at the end of the long corridor.

"Ah, shit," Nancy muttered then took off running.

And of course, Hurricane followed.

Nancy ran as fast as she could, and when she reached the double doors at the rear of the hospital that led out to the parking lot, she busted through them and into the night air. She looked over her shoulder. Hurricane was still coming at her and closing the gap fast.

THIRTY-FOUR

"HEATHER, DO THIS. HEATHER, DO THAT." Heather was always the good friend. The reliable friend. The friend who would sneak out in the middle of the night to pick up a friend from a hospital after who knew what. The friend who would just be cool about having her boyfriend stolen. Technically, Rick Gale wasn't her boyfriend, but she liked him, and Nancy knew that, so it was kind of the same thing. Heather was sick of being the good friend. When was it going to be her turn to make out with the Rick Gales of the world and to be the irresponsible one?

"When is my time!" she asked herself as she flicked on the indicator to pull off Old Randall Road toward the hospital.

Heather couldn't believe she was even driving out there in the middle of the night for her *best friend*.

What kind of friend was she?

She was angry at herself more than anything.

She pulled into the parking lot and saw Nancy, and when seeing her face made all the anger from the past few weeks bubble up, Heather slammed on the brakes.

"To hell with you, Nancy Sinclair," Heather said out loud. Then she slipped the car in reverse and drove home. She didn't even look back.

THIRTY-FIVE

NANCY WATCHED THE ROSSES' station wagon disappear down the street. "What the actual fuck, Heather?"

The car was gone. Heather was gone. And her escape was gone too.

Nancy turned, nice and slow. Just like she thought, Hurricane Williams was standing right behind her, towering over as she looked up into his bloodshot eyes that poked out through the hood.

He smelled something awful, like damp clothes and rotten eggs all rolled into one. Nancy would have dry retched if she weren't so terrified. It was the end of the line, and she knew it. She closed her eyes and waited for the end to come.

People say that in that last moment just before a person is about to die, their whole life flashes in front of them. Nancy's whole life didn't flash in front of her. Nancy thought about one thing and one thing only. She wished she had more time to fix all the things she had done wrong.

Then she heard a thump then a thud. Nancy's eyes snapped open.

The monster, the slasher, the gigantic Hurricane Williams was laid out flat on the ground. Standing behind him was Parker Ames, the girl Nancy knew as the psycho from Patrick's Garage & Gas.

Parker was holding an oxygen tank, which she'd just used to knock Hurricane out. "You've got about ten seconds before he gets up again, and when he does, he's going to be really cranky. If you want to keep all your arms and legs, come with me."

Hurricane was already starting to climb back up onto his feet, and the way Nancy saw her situation, she was all out of options. She followed Parker back into the hospital. They ran down the corridor, and although Nancy's knees hurt and her legs were tired, she kept up with Parker, who had barely broken a sweat.

When they reached the end of the hall, Parker slid to a stop just before they were about to take the corner. She looked over her shoulder and waited… and waited… and waited.

"What is that thing?" Nancy asked, panting for breath.

"Persistent," Parker said. "He's going to keep coming and coming until I can get my hands on some weapons."

"You don't have any weapons? Why don't you have any weapons?"

"Long story," Parker said.

"Maybe we should split up?"

"That never works out, trust me," Parker said, her eyes glued to the end of the hall.

"Maybe he'll gave up?"

"Did he look like the giving-up type to you?"

"No," Nancy said. "Not really."

And he certainly wasn't. Out of the darkness at the end of the hall, the dark figure appeared. With his machete in his hand, he thumped down that hall with the two girls in his sights.

"Time to go," Parker said, gripping Nancy's arm, and ran down a maze of corridors where they took left turns here and right turns there. Nancy wasn't sure that she would ever find her way back to the main entrance and the nurses' station.

They took a corner and ran straight, smack bang into Deputy Grady.

"Whoa, whoa, everybody slow down," he said. "What's happening?"

"He's coming!" Nancy yelled, pointing in the direction they just came from. "What do we do? What do we do! He's coming!"

"You need to calm down, Gidget," Parker said. "That's what you need to do."

Grady pulled his revolver. "I'll take care of this."

"Are you insane?" Parker asked, motioning to his revolver. "That's not going to stop him."

"Sweetheart," Grady said, "this bad boy would stop a Mack truck with just one round to the engine block."

Parker looked him up and down. "Good luck with that." She turned to Nancy. "I need my weapons; let's go."

"Shouldn't we stay with the police?"

"Not if you want to live."

Parker stepped off, so Nancy figured the discussion was off the table. She looked from Grady to Parker and weighed up her options. Should she stay, or should she go? To her in that moment, Grady looked like the cop the other cops send to go get coffee.

"Good luck," she said to Grady and followed Parker.

THIRTY-SIX

DEPUTY GRADY WATCHED THEM LEAVE. They weren't the first people who didn't take him seriously. In fact, nobody took Grady seriously at being a cop. Not his girlfriend or his sisters and certainly not his mother. They all treated him as if he were nine years old and playing dress up, but all he'd ever wanted to be was a cop, just like his old man.

Grady's father was a town hero around Happydale, and not because he was known to be a fair and honest cop who always gave people a fair and honest shake or because, at every Christmas, Grady, Sr. would dress up as Santa Claus and give out presents to the kids in the orphanage.

Grady, Sr. was a local hero because of one event and one event only. In 1953, when the old man was only in his second year of law enforcement, Grady got a phone call from Mrs. Miller up on Haddon Street, saying that she thought some kids had broken into the old Nester house. It had been abandoned since old man Nester had died sometime in '51. His two sons couldn't agree on whether or not to sell it, and because they couldn't agree, it'd sat empty for years. So Grady, Sr. climbed into his cruiser and headed on over to Haddon Street. He thought he would knock on the door, put the fear of God into a couple of teenagers, and head on back into town. That's what he thought anyway.

Grady pulled up to the old double-story house, which sat atop a slight hill like a cardboard cutout of a house in the old black-and-white horror movies he used to watch as a kid. The Nester house had fallen into disrepair over the few years it had been empty, and the floorboards on the porch had grown warped. When Grady, Sr. walked up the couple of steps and onto the porch, the boards creaked with each step he took.

Now what Grady, Sr. didn't know was that across state lines in Clovis, New Mexico, there was an all-points alert on the Eggleston gang. The gang consisted of four brothers—Howie, Daniel, Jake, and Ernest—and it was safe to say that none of the brothers were exactly the best the United States had to offer. The four of them had been in and out of one jail or another since they were ten years old, and six months ago, it'd just so happened to coincide that all four Eggleston brothers were out of the big house all at the same time, something which hadn't happened for thirteen years. They decided to celebrate by robbing the First National Bank in Tucson. They got away with that caper, so they robbed another bank in Los Alamos. In the previous two months, they had robbed six banks, stolen just shy of a million dollars, and murdered nine people, including two cops. They had been chased across three states and were lying low in the Nester house while Ernest recovered from a gunshot to the leg. Clearly, Grady, Sr. didn't know any of that when he knocked on the door alone and in full uniform. If he had, Grady, Sr. probably would have brought a few cops to back him up. As it turned out, he had taken Mrs. Miller at her word and assumed the only people in the Nester house were a bunch of teenagers goofing off.

When he knocked on the door, he certainly didn't expect to be met with a shotgun blast. He hit the deck armed with nothing more than the .45 on his hip and the nine bullets in the magazine. What Grady, Sr. did next made him a legend. He could have run or hidden, but he stayed and stood his ground. He kicked in what was left of that shotgunned door, and ninety seconds later, all four Eggleston brothers were as dead as nails. After that day, in the town of Happydale, Grady, Sr. never paid for a beer in his life.

That was the story Grady had in the back of his mind when he palmed his revolver and stepped into the path of Hurricane Williams. Grady checked the rounds in the revolver—all six were ready to rock 'n' roll. Grady leveled that big bastard up and took aim at the monster coming his way.

This will be my Nester house moment. They'll have to take me seriously now.

Grady waited until Hurricane was in range.

And waited…

And waited…

Hurricane wasn't deterred—he just kept on moving forward.

Grady wrapped his finger around the trigger. He drew a breath.

Hurricane kept on coming.

Sweat rolled down Grady's cheek.

Then finally, Hurricane was within shooting range. Grady squeezed the trigger and fired. *Bang! Bang! Bang! Bang! Bang! Bang!*

The slasher hit the deck. He was out cold and not moving.

Grady cocked his head; even he was surprised. He smiled and gave himself a little self-congratulatory nod as he half strutted, half walked down the corridor. *I did it*, he thought to himself. He was finally out of his father's shadow. He was no longer Roy Grady's boy. He was his own man.

Then Grady went and did what no one should ever do around a slasher. He walked up to Hurricane Williams and tapped him with his foot, to see if he really was dead.

Big mistake.

Hurricane grabbed hold of Grady's leg and ripped it clean off his body. Clean. Off. His. Body.

Naturally, Grady hit the deck, screaming, yelling, and moaning as Hurricane climbed to his feet, with Grady's leg still in his hand. Hurricane looked down at the three-limbed cop, who was still screaming, and beat him over and over with his own leg until Grady stopped screaming and his face was nothing but mush. And even then, he kept on beating.

THIRTY-SEVEN

PARKER AND NANCY heard the gunfire and didn't look back. They pushed though the double doors and stepped out into the parking lot.

"Do you think he's all right?" Nancy asked.

Parker scanned the parking lot, looking for a set of wheels. "Who?"

"The cop."

"Fuck no," she said. There were maybe a dozen or so cars in the parking lot, and half of them looked as if they'd been dumped there. "Let's find some wheels and get the hell out of here."

THIRTY-EIGHT

EVERYBODY IN TEXAS HAD A GUN, so when Jessica Hopkins heard gunfire in the hospital, she knew exactly what it was and hit the deck of the nurses' station. Irene had just come back from checking in on Nancy Sinclair and found her missing. Jessica figured the gunfire and the missing girl were not a coincidence.

Quietly and in slow motion, Jessica raised her hand and patted the desktop until her fingers latched onto the phone receiver. She pulled it down and put it to her ear then reached back to feel for the buttons to dial 911.

It rang.

And rang.

And rang.

The 911 call was automatically directed to the

Happydale police station, and although she didn't know it, the place was empty, except for Morrison lying facedown on the floor in a pool of his own blood. Nobody was answering that phone.

"What's happening?" Irene whispered.

"It's ringing," Jessica whispered back. "I don't think there's anyone there."

The Happydale Police answering machine kicked in, and Jessica left a message with all the pertinent details. "Gunfire. Hospital. Come now!" And she hung up.

"Do you think they'll come?" Irene asked.

"Sure," Jessica said, but she wasn't so sure. "Let's get out of here."

She rose to her feet, and when she did, Hurricane Williams was standing in the lobby, staring straight at her. He wasn't looking at something behind her; he wasn't looking at something next to her. He was looking straight through her, as if he could see into her soul and put the fear of God into everything there. He was as still as a statue and barely even moved when he breathed.

Jessica, on the other hand, was too scared to move. She was even too scared to look down at the machete in his hand, but she forced herself to do it anyway. Just as slowly as she'd looked down at the blade, she looked back into his bloodshot eyes again.

It took every single ounce of guts that she had to open her mouth and speak. When she finally did, her voice was nothing much louder than a whisper. "I'm not the one you want."

Hurricane cocked his head and looked at her as if those words were sinking in. Then Hurricane shifted his gaze from Jessica to the double doors that led out of the hospital, and his big heavy feet thumped down the hall. He pushed through the doors with his chest and stepped out into the night. The doors closed, and a couple of seconds after that, it was as if he had never been there to begin with.

"And you say nothing ever happens in this town," Irene said.

Jessica picked up the phone and dialed 911 again. "We need to find Jenko."

THIRTY-NINE

PARKER'S WHEELS turned out to be a 1956 Chevy. She found the beast of chrome and fire-red paint in the driveway of a double-story house about a mile away from the hospital.

As Parker and Nancy cut across the open yard, Parker snatched one of the old steel hangers from the line, and when they sidled up to the Chevy, Parker straightened the hanger and slipped the wire between the glass and the rubber seal on the driver's-side door. A moment later, she gave it a little yank, and when she pulled the hanger up, the button to the door popped open. Within a second or two, Parker was in the car, under the dashboard, and fiddling with wires. It wasn't the first car Parker had hotwired, and it certainly wouldn't be the last. One thing was for sure, though—it certainly was one of the easiest.

"Where'd you learn these things?" Nancy asked.

Parker had a quick flashback to McCormick taking her to junkyards in the middle of the night and teaching her how to break into cars and turn them over using nothing but her fingers. She must have hotwired over two thousand cars with McCormick.

She tapped two wires together, and the car roared to life. "I've had a little practice."

They climbed in and hit the road.

"We've got to go to the police," Nancy said.

"They're dead."

"What?"

"Dead," Parker said. "As in not breathing."

"All of them?"

"Pretty sure."

"So now what are we going to do?" Nancy asked. "We can't just drive around."

"We're not just driving around," Parker said as she pulled the Chevy into the main street of Happydale. And calling it a main street was a stretch. Parker was looking at two or three blocks of stores, most of which were out of business, and the ones that were still open wouldn't be far behind them. "We're looking for something."

"Another cop, I hope."

"There it is," Parker said as she hit the brakes right in front of Miller's Hardware.

"What are we doing *here*?" Nancy asked.

"Shopping."

Miller's Hardware was one of the oldest stores in Happydale, which put it high in the running to being one of the oldest stores in Texas. Old Man Miller, who owned and operated Miller's Hardware, was so old that the younger kids used to joke that he was the original Miller who'd first opened the store in 1806. Like most family businesses, Miller's Hardware had been handed down from father to son, and for six generations the family had always prided itself on running a business that brought value to the town. If someone needed a hammer, they went to Miller's. If they needed a shovel, they went to Miller's. It was Happydale's go-to for every hardware need. That was until a Home Depot opened up in the Cedar Springs mall. For over one hundred and seventy years, Miller's Hardware had looked after the town of Happydale. It'd provided the tools that built Happydale's homes, that plowed its farms, and cut its lawns. That was until a thirty percent discount on cleaning products came along that old man Miller couldn't match. At first, he didn't notice the dwindling sales. It was only a few bucks here and a few bucks there, but all those bucks added up, and a couple of years later, Old Man Miller was only making enough to keep the lights on and the TV dinners in his freezer.

Parker rattled the door. It was locked.

"We should probably knock," Nancy said.

Parker lifted her leg and karate kicked the door open. Wooden splinters flew everywhere. The door bounced against a stopper, hit the broken doorframe, and opened again.

Parker looked over her shoulder at Nancy. "Still want to knock?"

"Seems a little redundant now."

The smell of wood and oil filled Parker's nostrils as she stepped inside the hardware store. To a normal person, the tools lining the walls would have been the regular everyday tools for chopping wood and building houses, but to Parker Ames, they were weapons. Chain saws, axes, and hammers, all shiny and brand-new, lined the walls and glinted in the moonlight.

"Let's go shopping," Parker said.

And just as they were about to step inside and arm themselves to the teeth, Parker heard a sound right behind her. She stopped dead in her tracks.

They were footsteps and for a woman in the busi-ness of hunting slashers, footsteps in the dead of night were very rarely a good thing. Parker slowly turned, preparing herself for the hideous and frightening sight of Hurricane Williams, but it wasn't Hurricane Williams that she saw.

It was Dr. Jeremiah Ellis, with a revolver in his shaky hand.

FORTY

TO GET to Happydale as soon as humanly possible, Ellis sped through the Texas night with the roof of his red MG down just to keep him alert. His hair stuck out in all directions, making him look crazier than he typically did, but he didn't care. It wouldn't matter anyway; none of it would matter. All that did matter was that he get to Happydale and bring Parker Ames in himself.

It was one hell of a story. There was no doubting it—Jeremiah Ellis was going to write another book, and it was going to put him right back on top again. The damn thing practically wrote itself: all-American girl with a tragic past fantasizes about demonic, unkillable killers then goes on a killing spree out of a delusional sense of justice and revenge. It didn't hurt that she was blond, young, and pretty, and with her face on the cover, he was going to sell a million copies easy.

Hello, *New York Times* Best Seller List.

Hello, Hollywood adaptation.

Hello, Sally Jessy Raphael.

Parker Ames was going to be the biggest thing in serial killing since the Manson family. He could barely contain the smile on his face. He knew it was wrong. He knew it was awful and cruel, but for a brief moment, he hoped that it was bad in Happy-dale. He hoped it was really bad. He hoped there were bodies everywhere and that Parker Ames's fingerprints were all over them. The more horrific the events, the bigger the story would be.

It was an awful thought, and he knew it, so he pushed it out of his mind and let it play around in his subconscious.

When he arrived in Happydale, the first place he drove to was the Happydale Police Station, where he found one hell of a mess. There was blood all over the concrete path that led up to the doors of the station, and once Ellis hesitantly pushed through the door, he found some cop in a pool of his own blood.

Ellis doubled over and vomited into a half-empty trash can by a desk. "Christ," he mumbled to himself. "What a mess."

Without so much as a second thought, Ellis ran

out to his car, popped the trunk, and found his revolver wrapped up in an old shirt. He hadn't fired it in years, but if there was ever a time for a comeback, Ellis figured that time had come.

Happydale wasn't a big town. Sooner or later, the trail of dead bodies would end up at the local hospital, one way or another. Ellis climbed behind the wheel of his MG and sped off in the direction of Happydale Medical with the massive map of Texas spread out over the steering wheel and half the dashboard. He kept one eye on the road and one eye on the map and steered with his knees. He'd never been any good with maps. His second ex-wife always used to tell him that he must have been a spinning top in a previous life because he could never tell which way was up.

Then out of the one eye he had on the road, he saw a flash of blond hair run across the street of what he took to be the main drag of Happydale. He eased off the gas and stared into the night.

Yep, he thought. *It was her all right. It was Parker Ames.*

He pulled the car over to the side of the road, grabbed his revolver, and climbed out.

FORTY-ONE

"DR. ELLIS?" Parker asked as she squinted in the dark to see the revolver and the shaky hand that held it. "I totally didn't expect to see you just as I turned around."

"I've come to take you back, Parker."

"I'm a little busy right now. Can you come back a little later?"

"Your reign of horror is done here!" he said with an authority that didn't quite ring true. "How many more people have to die, Parker? How many people!"

Parker shook her head. "You idiot. You goddamn stupid idiot. Do you really think little old me is the one who's going around killing all these bastards?"

"I'm not going to buy into your fantasy, Parker. There are no such thing as 'slashers.' They're not coming to kill you. You're sick. Do you understand? But I can help you. I can make you better. No more people need to die here tonight. What do you say? Do you want to come with me?"

"No, idiot," Parker said. "I'm not going with you."

Ellis's shaky finger wrapped around the trigger of his revolver. "Then I'm sorry. There's no other way to end this evil."

Dr. Ellis pulled the trigger.

NOTE FROM THE PUBLISHER

DUE TO A PRINTING error of the last known 1989 copy of *Escape from Happydale*, which was the source for the current edition that you now hold in your hands, the pages between 172 and 204 were tragically lost. Fans have long speculated as to the content of the missing pages, which many believe referenced a previous Parker Ames novel, *Escape from Hell*, where she goes to hell and tries to kill the devil. Although we exhausted every avenue to obtain the missing pages and the previous novel and were unsuccessful, we cannot confirm the validity of the speculations.

We apologize for any inconvenience.

SIXTY ONE

MILLER'S HARDWARE was engulfed in flames as Parker dragged Dr. Ellis out of the burning building. He was in a bad way. Parker had seen people in bad ways before, but he took the cake. Hurricane had slammed a chain saw right through his belly until it came out the other side, and then the maniac had turned it on.

Ellis coughed blood. "They're real? They're real?" He kept saying it over and over again, as if the idea were too big for his mind to comprehend. He wrapped a bloody hand around the back of her head and pulled Parker close. "It's all up to you now," he slurred. "It's all up to you to stop him."

He took half a breath, then his body just stopped on him. As if he were on pause, his eyes were open and staring at nothing in particular over Parker's shoulder. Even though she knew she should climb to her feet and run like hell, Parker stayed there with him for a moment and just held his hand. But in the world of monsters and slasher girls, time really was of the essence.

"Parker!" Nancy yelled from the sidewalk. She was covered in soot and tears. "I think it's time for us to go." And she pointed into the fiery storefront.

Hurricane Williams was on fire, and he was walking through the burning store toward them as if he weren't.

"No," Parker said as she rose to her feet. "This ends now."

She gripped the machete in her hand, shifted her body weight so that her feet were planted squarely on the ground, and lined the burning slasher up in her sights.

She swung her shoulder back, and like she had ten thousand times before, she threw the machete. It cut through the air and the smoke in big whooshing sounds, aimed right for Hurricane's flaming skull.

Then at the last minute, either she moved, or he moved. Or her aim might have off. The machete changed course, and instead of hitting him square in the skull, the machete buried itself in Hurricane's shoulder.

It didn't even slow him down. He just kept coming.

"I guess this doesn't end now," Parker said to herself.

"Come on!"

Jessica and Irene had already bailed out of Happydale in Parker's stolen Chevy, and although she was glad that they were safe, she and Nancy were without a set of wheels at a time when they absolutely needed a set of wheels.

Without any other choices on the table, running was the only option they had left.

Parker looked over her shoulder at the worn-down, beat-down drive-in across the road. "We need a ride."

And they took off running.

SIXTY TWO

HURRICANE KNEW they were out there. The fire was out, but he was still smoking. He scanned the handful of vehicles that were scattered around the parking lot.

The Happydale Drive-In had been struggling for years, but it wasn't until they officially announced its closure six months ago that people started using it as a dumping ground. Most notably a dumping ground for stolen cars. By the look of most of the forgotten vehicles, they had been taken by kids, trashed around for a few hours and dumped in in front of the decaying screen. Some had smashed windows, others had scuffs all around the paint-work, and there was even a 1973 Mach 1 that had been set on fire and was now nothing more than a burned-out shell.

Hurricane knew they were out there, somewhere, hiding.

They always hid.

Nobody could run forever, and it was when they hid that he struck the fiercest. The slasher gripped his machete and slowly began working his way through the parking lot checking the back seats of the vehicles he passed.

The first few came up empty, and then there was a thump.

A small thump. A quiet thump. Something that would go unnoticed by any normal person. But Hurricane Williams wasn't a normal person. He was a slasher, and slashers paid attention to things that went thump.

Slowly the slasher turned his head, searching for the cause of the sound. His gaze settled on a Ford Galaxy. Even though he was wearing a mask, there was a very good chance that underneath that mask, Hurricane was smiling.

He had them.

His steps were slow and cautious as he made his way toward the Galaxy.

The inside was dark and what light there was came from the moon and that bounced off the rear window and showed only Hurricane's reflection as he neared the vehicle.

The slasher gripped the machete and held it high and ready to strike.

Hurricane was just about to slam that machete straight through the rear window and slash the living out of the girls in the back seat when at the very last minute he stopped dead in his tracks.

The back seat was empty. There's nothing on it except leather and old bottles of Shiner Bock.

Hurricane lowered the blade with a hint of disappointment. He walked past a Volkswagen Beetle, and the search continued.

Hurricane moved through the parking lot in search of his victims, then he heard the clunk. His head snapped back to the Beetle. There was no mistaking it this time. He knew where the sound was coming from.

SIXTY THREE

PARKER AND NANCY were hiding in the front seat of the Beetle, being all quietlike. Well, Parker was being quiet. Nancy was trying her best, but the night was starting to catch up with her, and to stop her from crying and screaming, Parker had to hold her down and hold her hand over her mouth. She struggled to break free, and when she did, her foot hit the glove box. Parker and Nancy froze. It was bad—real bad— and they both knew it.

Hurricane's footsteps grew louder as they pounded their way toward the Beetle.

The only weapon Parker had were her fists, and her fists were pretty good against regular, normal, non-slasher types. Against Hurricane Williams, they were about as powerful as a wet sock, and she knew it.

When Hurricane Williams appeared in the window, Nancy gasped, and Parker would have been lying if she said her legs hadn't turned to jelly.

This is not the way I go out, Parker thought to herself. After everything she had been though—all the battles, the fights, and downright craziness—she couldn't go out in the front seat of a Beetle. But when Hurricane Williams pulled open the door to the car, being stabbed to death in the front seat of a Beetle seemed exactly like the way she was going to go out.

Suddenly, she heard an engine rev up. Then headlights flashed. Out of nowhere, a car plowed right through Hurricane and sent him flying across the drive-in. In midair his limbs flopped around, his machete slipped from his fingers and after twenty or so feet of this acrobatic flight, Hurricane Williams hit the concrete hard and fast, and he didn't stop rolling until his head and massive body hit the side of an abandoned Mustang, putting a dent in its door and probably putting one in Hurricane also.

Parker climbed out of the Beetle and saw the slasher all the way on the other side of the drive-in, with his body all disjointed and not moving a muscle.

Then she shifted her attention to the vehicle that had sent Hurricane to flight school. It was a '68 F-100, and behind the wheel was a very gray-looking Sheriff Jenko.

"You girls need a lift?"

Parker cocked her head. "Aren't you supposed to be dead?"

"I don't feel too dead."

"Really?" Parker said. "You have looked better."

On the concrete, Hurricane was starting to move. His disjointed body was bending back into shape with god-awful cracking sounds that could be heard even with the distance between them.

"Do you ladies want to hop inside, or do you want to hang out with your new best friend over there?" Jenko asked.

Nancy didn't need to be told twice; she climbed into the truck in two shakes of a lamb's tail.

Parker, on the other hand, had other ideas. She wanted what Hurricane wanted. She wanted to go toe-to-toe and tear him apart.

"Hey, sweetheart," Jenko said. "Choose your battles. Something tells me he will find you, and when he does, make sure you're holding something more in your hands than just your fists."

Jenko was right.

See you around, she thought to herself as she gave Hurricane one last look before climbing into the truck and hanging on as Jenko floored it out into the street.

Parker looked at Nancy. "Are you okay?"

"We're all going to die, aren't we?"

"Not unless we all adopt that positive attitude of yours." She shifted her attention to Jenko. "What about you?"

Jenko moved his hand away from his belly to reveal a bloody wound in his gut. "He got me good."

"Are you going to die?"

His face scrunched up like an old newspaper. "You might want to work on your bedside manner, Parker."

"You're no good to us dead."

"I've called for backup. Cliff Moore and a couple of deputies are coming over from Cedar Springs. They should be here within an hour."

Parker leaned back in the seat, cracked the window, and let the breeze cool the sweat on her brow. "Just get me to my weapons."

SIXTY FOUR

THERE WERE no two ways about it—Jenko should have been dead. He should have been lying on the sidewalk outside the Happydale police station with a hole in his gut and his soul in heaven. When Gordon's head had smashed through the window at the station, Jenko had been pretty sure he was dealing with a 100% certified, genuine off-his-rocker psycho. That he was certain of. What he wasn't anticipating was that said psycho in question was damn near superhuman. After they'd exhausted all avenues to solve the situation with a dialog and it'd become apparent that wasn't going to work, they tried to detain the suspect. That was when all hell broke loose.

Jenko had never seen anything like it. Pure. Animal. Force.

Hurricane swatted Morrison away like he was a fly, and when the psycho tried to ram a machete through the deputy, that's when Jenko had no other choice but to open fire on him. It wasn't the first time Jenko had aimed a weapon at somebody and pulled the trigger.

After Nam, he didn't even like to think about the amount of times he had done it, and even though people said it gets easier to live with over time, Jenko knew from experience that it absolutely did not get easier. If he thought about the things he had done in combat, about the fathers, and brothers, and sons he had taken, all he had to do was close his eyes, and there they were.

It was always the same setting. He was in his backyard, having a cookout, with the grill going and the beer flowing, and he could smell his grandfather's secret chili sauce. But instead of friends, family, and neighbors, the people in the yard were the people he had killed. They were all staring at him, and they were all asking him the exact same question. *Why?*

He didn't know the answer any more than he knew why the sky was blue and water was wet. What he did know was that when he got back to civilian life, he wasn't going to aim a weapon at anybody ever again. In the event that he had to, if there was no other choice but to unholster his side arm and wrap his finger around the trigger, there was no chance in hell he was going to squeeze that trigger without being absolutely, positively, one hundred and ten percent sure that whoever was on the receiving end deserved it.

So when Hurricane raised his machete high into the sky and moonlight bounced off its blade, Jenko made that evaluation on whether or not he should pull that trigger and when the time came, Jenko didn't think twice and squeezed. He fired three rounds into the chest of Hurricane Williams, and for a brief moment, he thought he had him and that it was just a bloody end to a bloody night. But that wasn't the end of it. Not by a long shot.

Hurricane came at Jenko like a wounded beast. Jenko fired off three more rounds. Two went wild, and the third hit Hurricane in the shoulder. It didn't slow him down at all, though. He just kept on charging.

Jenko pulled the trigger—and heard nothing but the *click, click, click* of an empty weapon, and before Jenko could run, hide, or reload, Hurricane pulled back his shoulder and slashed at Jenko's belly. He stepped back, tripped, and slipped, and when he fell, Jenko hit his head on the concrete and was knocked out cold.

What happened next, Jenko pieced together from the aftermath. He didn't know how long he was out, but when he woke, there was blood all over the sidewalk, Morrison was lying dead on the station floor, and Parker Ames was gone. He patched up the wound on his belly from the first-aid kit they kept under the kitchen sink and took a shot of whiskey from the emergency bottle he kept in the bottom drawer.

The wound in his side was bad. Another hour lying on the sidewalk, and he would have been dead. He stopped the bleeding with a field dressing and figured that he would most likely be okay for the time being. He took another shot of whiskey, and as he put the bottle down, he saw the flashing light of the answering machine.

His bloody finger pressed Play, and Jessica Hopkins's voice came on the machine. There had been shooting down the hospital, and they needed help pronto.

He'd grabbed a box of ammo and walked out to find Parker Ames.

With Nancy and Parker in the car, he was headed back to the station to bunker down and wait for Cliff Moore and their back up that should be arriving as soon as humanly possible from Cedar Springs.

Jenko brought the cruiser to a stop just outside the

station. He climbed out, looked up and down the street, saw it was empty in both directions, and told Nancy it was safe to open the door. She stayed close to his side as the three of them walked into the station. It was exactly how they'd left it. The lights were still on, Parker's weapons were still on the desk, and Morrison's corpse was still face down on the floor.

Parker and Jenko stepped straight on past it; they had both seen it before and the shock was lost on them the second time around. But for Nancy, it was the first time, and she stopped and looked down in horror.

"Oh, my God." she said. "There's another body here? What the fuck?"

"There's going to be three more if you don't get your shit together." Parker pointed to a chair. "Now sit down and get your shit together."

She sat as Jenko made his way to the weapons locker, unlocked it with a key from his pocket, pulled out a shotgun, and started loading shells into it.

"Your guns are useless against him," Parker said as she picked up the ax from the table of her confiscated gear. "You'd be better off with something a little more primitive," she said. holding up the ax.

Jenko wasn't convinced. "I think I'll keep the boomstick."

"Suit yourself," she said but added under her breath, "But don't come crying to me when you've been brutally murdered." She handed the ax to Nancy. "Gidget, I guess the ax is all yours."

When Nancy took it from Parker, the ax almost slipped from her hands. "I don't know how to use it."

"You swing," Parker said.

"What if I don't know how to swing?"

"Then you die."

Nancy let those words sink in as Jenko slipped his fingers between the blinds and looked out the window at the dark and quiet street. He'd seen that view of the sleepy town of Happydale for years. But that night was the first night he'd looked into the shadows, and instead of seeing a small innocent town asleep for the evening, he saw horror and fear in those shadows, and a night with no end.

He saw hell coming.

"Who is this son of a bitch?" Jenko asked, letting the blinds snap back into place.

"That son of a bitch out there is Hurricane Williams, and he's clearly a son of a bitch you don't want after you," Parker said.

"What's he want?" Nancy asked.

"To kill," Parker said to Nancy. "More specifically, he wants to kill little ol' me and little ol' you."

"Me?" Nancy scoffed. "What did I ever do?"

"It's not what you did," she said. "It's what our parents did."

Nancy frowned, trying to make sense of everything. "What did our parents do?"

"There are some men out there," Parker said, "that are so evil, not even hell wants them." Piece by piece, Parker unwrapped her weapons from the evidence bags on the desk as she told her story. "Ten years ago, your father, Adrian Sinclair, headed up a team of military scientists studying the effects of sleep deprivation on soldiers."

"And what were those effects?" Jenko asked.

"They weren't good," Parker replied. "I can tell you that much. You see, these assholes wanted to keep three soldiers awake for thirty days. The poor bastards who volunteered for this god-awful experiment were locked in a sealed bunker-like environment while an experimental gas was pumped in along with the oxygen, and this gas was supposed to stop them from falling asleep."

"Did it?" Nancy asked.

"It did. For five days, everything was just hunky-dory," Parker continued. "The soldiers would laugh and joke and play cards, but on the sixth day, something happened. They stopped talking to each other. Each of them would huddle into different corners of the bunker and whisper to themselves."

"Whisper?" Jenko said. "What did they say?"

"Nobody knew," Parker replied. "Then on the ninth day, the screaming started. One by one, the soldiers screamed at the top of their lungs, and this screaming went on for the next three days. Then suddenly, on the fourth day, it simply stopped. Just like that, they heard zip. At first, they didn't know why they had all shushed up, then logic kicked in, and they came to the realization that the three poor bastards had torn their vocal cords."

Parker paused and let the silence linger in the air for a moment.

"Then what happened?" Nancy asked.

"After twenty-nine days, somebody must have thought it was probably a good idea to end the experiment. They flushed the gas out of the bunker and stepped inside. What they found would chase each and every one of them for the rest of their lives. Two of the subjects were dead. It appeared they had torn their own organs out of their bodies while they were still alive."

"And the third subject?" Jenko asked.

"As it turns out, that third subject wasn't all that happy. He tore everybody to shreds." Parker paused. "Every. Body. To. Shreds," she said again. "He ripped the throat out of one of the soldiers, the testicles off another, and every single other person who stood in his way was torn apart limb by bloody limb. Those who survived…"

"Our fathers?" Nancy asked.

"They were among them," Parker said. "Those who survived renamed Private Williams Hurricane Williams because of the amount of destruction he could inflict in a short amount of time. It wasn't too long until the police captured him, and he was rightfully sentenced to death row. Hurricane was scheduled to be executed late on a Friday night. They gave him five doses of lethal injection before he was clinically pronounced dead meat. It appears Hurricane had an aversion to death. He was taken to the morgue at midnight, and exactly an hour later, he walked out of that morgue, killing two doctors and a security guard."

Nancy leaned in closer. "He wasn't dead."

"Deadish?" Parker said. "Now Hurricane Williams walks the earth, looking for bloody revenge on everyone involved in his botched execution, and unless we stop him, he will get it."

For a long time, nobody said a word as they let that horrific story sink in.

"Horseshit," Jenko said. "You're full of fucking

horseshit. Three days ago, you were in a fucking mental asylum. I don't believe a word of it."

"Why were you in an asylum?" Nancy asked. "Why?"

"Because I believe there are monsters in the world, and some people thought that was crazy."

"I think that's crazy," Jenko said.

"Tell that to the corpse on the floor of your police station."

"He's not a goddamn monster," Jenko said. "He's just a man. Plain and goddamn simple. Like any other man out there."

Parker raised her eyebrow slightly.

"I can't be here," Nancy said and headed for the door. "I've got to go home."

Parker called out, and Nancy stopped and looked back. "There's nothing there for you anymore."

"How do you know that?"

"I've been to your house," Parker said.

Nancy looked over her shoulder at Parker, and in those words, she understood exactly what had happened. Her eyes started to well up, and tears rolled down her cheek.

"This sucks," Parker said. "Trust me, I know it sucks. Now, you can do one of two things." She held up a finger. "You can walk out that door and take your chances. Nobody will stop you." She held up a second finger alongside the first. "Or you can pick up a weapon and help me destroy this asshole."

Nancy picked up the ax. "Let's do it."

There was movement outside. Jenko sidled up to the window, separated a couple of the blinds with his two fingers, and saw a Cedar Springs prowler pull up outside the station.

"Cliff Moore and our backup from Cedar Springs is here," Jenko said. "We'll show that son of a bitch now."

SIXTY FIVE

CLIFF MOORE from Cedar Springs wasn't originally Cliff Moore from Cedar Springs at all, and in that current situation in Happydale, that was a good thing. In the beginning, Cliff Moore from Cedar Springs was Cameron Jones from Buffalo, New York. And the people of Buffalo had called him Buffalo Jones. Now Buffalo Jones was a known badass. His old man was a freelance hitman with a reported twenty-three murders under his belt. He'd died in prison when Buffalo was nine years old, so as a boy, Buffalo had known his father by way of reputation only. People would tell him that his old man was a stand-up guy and that he should do him proud. Buffalo didn't really know what that meant, but at the time, he'd thought that meant dropping out of school and using his fists instead of his brains to get by.

The year was 1942, and fifteen-year-old Buffalo had already started to make a name for himself. He was a big kid, bigger than most of the guys in their twenties. Most of that was due to genetics, but a lot more of it was due to the three hours that Buffalo Jones spent in the gym each morning. He'd read in a copy of *Ringside* that Jake LaMotta woke up at five o'clock every morning to train, so that was exactly what Buffalo did. He followed Jake LaMotta's training schedule to the letter, and some of the old timers in the neighborhood thought that maybe he could go pro. He'd thought about it—he really had—but in the end, he figured he would need trainers, promoters, backers, and a million other people with their hands in his pocket. Nope. To Buffalo Jones, there was a lot more money putting his specific skill set to use in other areas—specifically, crime.

He was a half-decent standover man. All he would have to do was stare at somebody for long enough with his cold blue eyes, and they would quickly fall into line. But what Buffalo loved more than anything else in the world was a good old fist-fight. Just standing there out on the street, going toe to toe with some big monster was the only time that Buffalo Jones felt at peace. Throwing punches and taking blows was the only time he truly felt he could be himself. The rest of the time, life was just make-believe.

Over his teenage years, Buffalo Jones made a name for himself, one that was out of the shadows of his old man, but the young heavy's life all came crashing down one night at Paddy's Pub. Buffalo was sitting at the bar one night, having a sarsaparilla—it was always a sarsaparilla, because back then, he didn't drink alcohol—when Frankie Fearless came in, looking to make a name for himself. Buffalo Jones was known as being the best street fighter in the city, and Frankie Fearless was known as being the second-best street fighter in the city. When Frankie walked into Paddy's Pub, he was looking to change that situation, and Buffalo was only too happy to put him back in his place.

At first, Buffalo Jones was only going to give him a hiding, maybe break an arm, nothing permanent, but something about Frankie Fearless got under his skin. Maybe it was the cocky way he walked into Paddy's. Maybe it was the entourage of assholes Frankie brought in with him. Whatever it was, Buffalo changed his mind about going easy on him. They went out to the alley behind Paddy's, Frankie Fearless threw the first punch, and that was the only punch he got in. Buffalo Jones went to work. He punched and pounded then pounded and punched, and after a quick flurry of punches, Frankie Fearless was out cold. The punches weren't what killed him. When he went down, Fearless cracked his skull on the concrete, and it was lights out. That was the end of it for Buffalo. He had never killed anyone before, and the experience didn't sit well with him. When he looked into Frankie's lifeless eyes, he knew he never wanted to hurt another soul again. He also didn't want to go to jail.

So Buffalo Jones changed his name to Cliff Moore, and he ran. He never stayed anywhere more than a year or two, and he never settled in anywhere. He spent a couple of years in Florida, where he picked up a couple of tours on a fishing boat, then he ran to Texas, where he spent a year on a cowboy ranch running beef all over the southern states. For twenty years, he ran all across the country, trying to hide from who he was, but when he stopped off in Cedar Springs, walked into Leonard's Diner, and laid eyes on Mary, he first danced with the idea of staying for more than five minutes. Mary was only thirty-one years old, but she looked as if she were forty-one. The look suited her, though. She was wise and sweet, and every afternoon, she made sure Crazy Larry who lived on the park bench across from Leonard's had a hot meal.

Buffalo picked up some day work down at the rubber factory, and every afternoon at four o'clock, after his shift ended, he went to Leonard's for a late lunch. He would stay until Mary closed up at six o'clock, and after three months of spending the afternoon with Mary, Buffalo finally worked up the courage to ask her to a movie. They saw *Jaws*, and afterward, as he walked her back to her father's house. Mary slipped her fingers in between his, and they walked very slowly as they held hands, making the walk last for as long as possible.

Three months later, they were married. Before they said their vows, Buffalo came clean and told her of his wild years. Mary listened with an open heart and an open mind, and when he was finished with all the horrible details of the things he had done and the life he had taken, he had tears streaming down his face. He expected the wedding to be over, for Mary to be disgusted and storm out. But Mary stayed. She made him promise her one thing: that he spend every day from that day onward trying to make the world a better place. And that was just he did. He started a homeless shelter, delivered meals to the elderly, and taught young girls self-defense. Every single day, he did one thing to help make the world a better place, and when he was fifty-five years of age, he ran for Sheriff of Cedar Springs. To his surprise, he won.

By the time the telephone rang at two in the morning, he had been living as Cliff Moore for decades and hadn't even uttered the name Buffalo Jones in years. It was as if Buffalo Jones was a whole other person that Cliff Moore had heard about through a friend of a friend. But after Jenko told him about the hell they had been living through over there in Happydale, he knew straight away that they didn't need Cliff Moore. They needed Buffalo Jones.

He climbed out of bed all quietly, so he wouldn't wake Mary, then he made his way downstairs to the kitchen. He made two phone calls: one to Deputy Ringo and the other to Deputy Sarrantonio. He told the pair of them to get their weapons, get into their vehicles, and meet him down at the station. He lived slightly farther out than his deputies, and when he arrived, they were waiting for him. Neither of them did the bitch-and-moan about the hour. They just reported for duty like the good soldiers they were.

Buffalo had inherited both Ringo and Sarrantonio when he was made sheriff. They were old-school. One hundred years ago, the pair of them, with their handlebar mustaches and six-shooters strapped to their hips, would have been chasing Billy the Kid all over Texas. And knowing them, they would have gunned him down in half the time that Pat Garrett did.

Between the three of them, they kept Cedar Springs on the straight and narrow. Not that the town was out of control with troubles like they had in the cities. It was nice and easy. A good place for three hard-asses to retire.

"Goddamn son of a bitch," Ringo said when Buffalo told him there was a madman on the run and murdering folks over there in Happydale.

Sarrantonio cursed himself for leaving Betsy, his favorite shotgun, at home. There wasn't time to go and get it, so he would have to make do with the Smith & Wesson on his hip. They all piled into Buffalo's prowler and hit the road. They kept the chatter to a minimum, which was just the way Buffalo liked it. Somewhere deep in his belly, he knew they were walking into a world of hell, and if he was going to survive that hell, he was going to have to leave Cliff Moore at home. Buffalo Jones was going to have to go to Happydale.

SIXTY SIX

TWENTY-FIVE MINUTES LATER, headlights lit up the inside of the Happydale police station. Jenko rose to his feet and peered through the blinds. When he saw that Cedar Springs Sheriff Department logo on the side of the car, relief washed over him.

He looked back at Parker and Nancy with a big shit-eating grin on his face. "Now we'll show that lunatic."

Parker wasn't so sure.

Jenko unlocked the three locks on the door and stepped out onto the porch of the station as Buffalo and his deputies climbed out of the car.

"We heard you had yourself a psychopath problem," Buffalo said.

Jenko nodded. "You heard right."

"No need to worry," Buffalo said as he racked his

shotgun. "You hear that, you mongrel? You came to the wrong fucking town and fucked with the wrong fucking people. Between me and the boys here, we've got over a hundred years of huntin' and fightin' and cursin' under our belts. We've scraped our knuckles on the teeth of some of the toughest sons of bitches God's green earth has to offer, and we've come out on top. Do you really think we're afraid of little old you?"

Jenko looked over his shoulder back at Parker as if to say, "These guys are going to save the day."

Parker wasn't as convinced.

"Now, you mongrel," Buffalo continued, "what the hell are you waiting for?"

Just on cue, a chain saw roared to life.

Parker jumped to her feet. "Get them inside now!"

Too late.

Out of the darkness, Hurricane Williams emerged, with his idling chain saw in his hand. Before anyone had a chance to do anything, he charged the group. It all happened too quickly.

Ringo didn't stand a chance. The chain saw ripped through his back and popped out the front of his chest, spraying blood all over Sarrantonio like a fountain.

It wasn't Hurricane's first chain sawing. He could

swing that machine around as if it weighed little more than a feather. He yanked it out of Ringo, and while Sarrantonio was still wiping the blood out of his eyes, Hurricane swung the machine right into Sarrantonio's neck. It cut into him with the ease of a knife cutting through butter until he hit the spine. At that point, the motor started to struggle, but the damage was done.

"Enough of this shit," Buffalo said. He yanked up his shotgun, wrapped his finger around the trigger, and squeezed.

Crack!

He'd missed. The blast went high and wide, just over Hurricane's shoulder.

"Damn it!" he snapped. He was out of practice, and it was most likely the last mistake Buffalo would ever make, because by the time Buffalo could rack another shell into the barrel, Hurricane buried the chain saw into the belly of the old street fighter. His body shook and convulsed, almost as if he were trying to get away, but with a chain saw stuck in his belly, Buffalo wasn't going anywhere.

Hurricane put his shoulder into it and pulled the machine from one side of Buffalo's side to the other, cutting him in half. In. Half.

The two halves hit the deck, and no longer tasked

with cutting through humans, the chain saw motor idled down to a gentle murmur.

Hurricane looked up from the carnage to Jenko and Parker up on the porch of the station. Jenko was as white as a ghost, with a look on his face that could've best been described as a "what the hell have I just seen" kind of a look.

Parker pulled him by the arm. "Come on. Let's go."

He didn't budge, but she pulled him again, a little harder, and Jenko finally took a couple of steps back into the station. Parker locked the door, and when she peered through the window, Hurricane Williams was gone, but someone like Hurricane Williams was never gone for good.

Jenko reached into the lowest drawer of his desk and pulled out his bottle of bourbon. His hands were shaking, and he didn't even bother with a glass. He pulled the cork off with his teeth, spat it aside, and swallowed a couple of gulps. He wiped his mouth with the back of his hand.

"Goddamn it," Jenko said. "I mean, goddamn it! He tore through those men like they were nothing." He muttered *goddamn* again under his breath a few more times, and his mind raced. He had been in the shit before. He'd lived through two tours in Vietnam. He had seen men on either side of him fall. He had survived some of the worst, scariest situations a man could be in, but none of that compared to what he'd just witnessed.

Goddamn, he thought. Moore, Ringo, and Sarrantonio weren't rookies. Ringo and Sarrantonio were seasoned lawmen. They came from a long tradition of seasoned lawmen. Jesus, Ringo's granddaddy had even chased Butch Cassidy out of the country, and that thing out there had just torn through them within seconds.

Jenko slumped into the chair behind his desk. *How the hell did I get into this shit?*

All of a sudden, Jenko's future didn't look too promising. He wasn't a fool; he knew people didn't live forever. He knew that sooner or later, people packed it in and faded from whatever this world was. He had seen both his parents die: one of cancer, the other of bad luck. He had seen countless guys die in the war, but he wasn't in the war anymore. He was back, and he figured he would have a couple of more decades left. Now that he was a father, he realized how badly he wanted those years. He wanted to see his boy, Jacob, take his first steps, say his first words, and throw his first baseball. He wanted to tell him all the things his father had never told him. Jenko wanted to shield his son from all the horrors of the world and show him all the good things, like freshly baked pie, warm summer mornings, and what it's like to win after failing. He wanted to be a part of Jacob's life. As he thought about all that, Jenko realized there was a very good chance that the next few minutes of his life may very well be his last.

What chance did he really have? He weighed up all those options in his mind as he looked out the window at the hacked-up lawmen in the street then at the two girls in his station, and he was doing the math, but the math didn't add up. He wasn't going to survive the night. Not against that maniac. He knew that much. Not unless he was going to do something drastic.

And drastic was just what he did. Jenko climbed to his feet, palmed his weapon, raised that big heavy son of a bitch, and took aim at Nancy Sinclair.

Poor Nancy, she didn't know what the hell was going on.

"Sweetie," Jenko said to her, "it's time for you to leave."

Parker looked over, saw what was happening, and took slow and very cautious steps over to the developing situation. "Jenko? Do you mind explaining what's going on here?"

"Yeah, I'd like to know too," Nancy said.

"You've got to go," Jenko said. "You've both got to go."

"I don't want to go," Nancy said.

"No one's going anywhere, okay," Parker said. "So everybody just be cool." She looked at Jenko. More specifically, she looked at the revolver in his hand. "Which means you need to lower that hand cannon in your hand."

"Goddamn, I hate doing this," he said. "I'm not proud right now, but I've got a little boy, and he needs a daddy. And that… that thing out there. He doesn't want me. He wants you. Both of you. You said so yourself. I send you out, and everybody goes home happy."

"Not everybody," Nancy said.

"Well, I do," he said. "Now, very slowly and without any sudden movements, get the goddamn hell out of my station. The pair of you."

"That's not going to happen," Parker said to Nancy, trying to reassure her.

Jenko shifted his aim to Parker. "You, little girly, don't have much of a say in the matter."

"Is that so?" Parker said.

"That is."

Parker took a couple more steps—again, very slowly and full of caution so as not to spook the sheriff with a gun. She didn't stop until she was standing between Nancy and Jenko like some sort of human shield.

"I'm going to give you to the count of three before you and I are going to have some problems," Parker said.

Jenko pulled back the hammer on the revolver—the universal symbol that one is simply not fucking around. "No. I'm going to give you to the count of three to walk out that door and into the night."

"Is that so?"

"That is," Jenko said. And then he started his count. He drew a breath, and when almost all the air was out of his lungs, he said, "One."

Quicker than a gunslinger, Parker drew her .45 and aimed that deadly bastard dead center in between Jenko's eyes. Then she pulled the trigger.

SIXTY SEVEN

THE ROUND EXPLODED out of Parker's gun. Jenko was dead before he even hit the deck.

"What the shit!" Nancy yelled. "You just killed a cop. A cop! What happened to counting to three?"

Parker holstered her still-warm .45. "Either he was going to die, or we were going to die."

"You don't know that. How do you know that? He might have changed his mind."

"Did he look like he was going to change his mind?"

Nancy paused and thought about it. "No."

"Then case closed."

But it wasn't case closed for Parker. Not really anyway. *Why did he have to go and do something stupid like that?* Parker thought as she looked at his body slumped over a desk. *Beau Jenko, you stupid bastard.*

He would be another face she saw when she closed her eyes late at night before she went to sleep. Another face to haunt her dreams. Another person she couldn't bring back even if she wanted to. The way she saw it, it was him or her, and she was damned sure it wasn't going to be her. That didn't make it any easier, though. There was nothing that would make it easier. Out of all the innocent people Parker had seen killed over the years, Beau Jenko was one of the ones who deserved it the least.

Parker took a couple of steps over to the window and scanned the dark street. She was used to scanning dark streets for monsters and could usually see within half a second if something was there or not. The street was clear, but that didn't mean Hurricane wasn't close by, just waiting to jump out of the darkness.

"We need to get the hell out of here," Parker said.

"What do you suggest?" Nancy snapped. "We can't go out there. Everyone that goes out there ends up dead."

The blood, and the bodies, and the killing were all second nature to Parker. She sometimes forgot what it was like to be a normal everyday person one minute and to be running for your life the next. Parker took Nancy's hand and led her to a chair, and they sat.

"I know you're real scared," she said. "But sooner or later—and let's be clear, most likely sooner rather than later—Hurricane is going to get in here, and I guarantee you, as soon as he does that, you'll wished that you got the fuck out of here as soon as you had the chance."

"What if…" Nancy said. "What if…"

"There are no more what-ifs," Parker said. "We leave here, or we die. Across the street is the Dodge Charger that I drove here in. It's got a full tank of gas, a Magnum 440 V8 under the hood, and a hell of a lot of grunt. Now here's what's going to happen. I'm going to walk out that door, walk across the yard to where my stolen car is, crank that car up, and be back here in under ninety seconds. You jump inside, and we hightail it out of here and live to fight another day."

"Why do we have to fight another day?" Nancy asked. "Why can't we just do the 'live' part?"

"He'll find us again," Parker said. "He'll always find us. I'm going to get you out of this. I promise."

Nancy looked at the floor. It was a hell of a lot for her to take it. Then she looked back up at Parker. "What do you want me to do?"

"I want you to stay here and be real cool, okay?" She slapped her .45 into Nancy's palm. "If you hear anything, fire off a round. If you see anything, fire off a round. If something comes at you, you run, and you never look back… Are we clear?"

Nancy looked down at the weapon in her hand. "Clear."

"Then let's get down to business," Parker said as she pulled the plastic evidence bag off Aerosmith and cranked that beast up. Originally, Aerosmith was covered in bright orange, but Parker had pulled it apart, customized, and spray painted that bad boy black. Holding it in her hand was like pulling on a favorite sweater; it just felt right. The tank was full of gas, and when it idled, it sounded like a mean bastard dog growling in the dark. Training with McCormick felt like a million years ago to Parker. A lot had happened since then. Friends and lovers had come and gone. Some of them were dead. Some of them were just gone. One thing that remained consistent throughout those years—Parker really did love to use a chain saw to send slashers back to hell.

She made it as far as the door of the station, and she had her free hand around the handle when Nancy called to her.

"Thank you," the girl said.

Parker smiled. "I don't hear that often in my line of work."

"Is that because everybody dies?" Nancy asked.

"Probably," she said. "I'll be back in a minute," she said as she stepped out into the night.

The Charger was parked on the other side of the road, about one hundred feet away, with its nose aimed in their direction. It wasn't exactly a huge distance, but considering Hurricane was out there, lurking in the shadows somewhere, it might as well have been ten miles between them. The street was quiet, and all Parker could hear was the chain saw *chug, chug, chug* in her hand. She scanned left to right and didn't see a thing. No stray cats roaming the street. Not even a breeze in the air. As clear as the coast may have looked, there was no point taking chances.

He was out there. She could feel it. She didn't know where. She'd rather not know where. She just had to get to the car, get the car back to Nancy, and get the pair of them the hell out of there.

She took slow step after slow step and kept her eyes peeled for the villain when…

Bang! A single shot rang out in the night.

Parker snapped her head back to the police station. Hurricane Williams was in the doorframe, towering over Nancy, and she was frozen with fear.

Parker knew from experience that when people froze in certain situations, situations such as the one

Nancy found herself in, drastic measures were needed to get the hell out of them.

Hurricane cranked up his chain saw. The thing roared and revved as he raised it high above his head. It was about to be all over Red Rover for Nancy.

"Hey!" Parker called out.

The slasher looked back over his shoulder at Parker.

"Why don't you leave her alone and come over here and settle this man to man, or girl to… whatever the fuck you are?"

Hurricane contemplated that option. He looked from Nancy to Parker and back again as if trying to decide between two impossible choices. He took one more look at Parker, revved his chain saw, and rammed it straight into Nancy's belly.

Parker yelled out, but there was no point. Nancy barreled over and hit the ground. That didn't stop Hurricane from going in for another blow. The chain saw went up, and it went down through Nancy's back, digging into the floorboards on the other side of her body. When he was finished, he pulled that chain saw out of the poor girl, stood defiantly over her, and stared Parker down, as if to say she was next.

Parker had told Nancy everything was going to

be all right. Nancy had believed her, and now she was dead.

"That," Parker said, pointing to Nancy. "That was unnecessary."

Hurricane didn't appear to care much about Parker's opinion as he came down the couple of steps and onto the sidewalk. He made his way toward Parker but stopped at a good pre-battling distance.

Parker wrapped her fingers around the handle of Aerosmith, gave him a quick few revs, and aimed the dangerous end at Hurricane. "I'm going to send you to hell," she said. "And then I'm going to go to hell and kill you all over again."

Hurricane Williams raised his murder weapon above his head in a war cry, then the pair engaged in a good, old-fashioned duel... with chain saws.

Hurricane stepped forward with one dirty boot after another, and Parker's cowboy boots took one step after the other as she faced off with her nemesis. The two warriors circled each other for a full 360 degrees.

The pair of them were just sussing each other out. Waiting. Biding their time. Sizing up their foes. Just waiting for that moment, that opening where one of them could make their first strike.

Then... an opening came. Hurricane swung. Hard and fast—down like an ax.

Parker blocked, and the chain saws jammed together, causing sparks to blast out everywhere.

They swung, and they clashed. They danced, and they separated like two old fighters in a grudge match. Parker was covered in sweat, and despite the exhaustion of the night and everything that had happened, she was one hundred percent in the zone, and just for a moment there, she thought that maybe, after all those years, just maybe she could do it.

That was all the energy Parker needed. It lit a fire in her belly, and she wasn't giving up. She wasn't running. Someone was going to hell, and Parker was going to fight her guts out to make sure it wasn't her.

Parker yanked the chain saw back and swung it forward. She missed the slasher completely, slipped, and lost her footing. Off balance, she spun around, and that's when Hurricane saw his chance and went in for the kill. He raised his machine high in the sky and was coming down hard, but Parker wasn't down for the count just yet. She blocked him. Their weapons locked together... entangled... Their faces drew close.

Hurricane lifted his knee up and pounded a big heavy boot into Parker's stomach and sent her flying back into the street. When she hit the ground, she couldn't breathe. Her chest felt like it had caved in on itself, and she gasped for air.

Instead of running in for the kill, Hurricane paused. He gave her a moment, toying with her like it was just sport for him.

Parker dragged as much air into her lungs as she could, and after a half a dozen or so of breaths, she rolled over onto her hands and knees. She spat blood and took her time climbing to her feet. She scraped Aerosmith up from the road and smiled a bloody smile.

"I'm not dead yet, you son of a bitch."

Enough was enough. No more playing. Hurricane charged toward her with his big heavy feet pounding on the road. Parker had nothing left. She could barely stand. She looked beaten, frail, and weak and in nowhere near any shape to fight off the hulking mass of slasher coming her way.

Parker gripped Aerosmith and closed her eyes. *Is this it?*

After everything she had been through, everything she had seen, it was all coming to an end with the very same monster that had put her on this path. On one hand, death would be peace to Parker Ames. No more dead bodies. No more fighting. No more monsters. No more horror. Then on the other hand… Parker Ames wouldn't die so easily.

Her bloodshot eyes snapped open. Hurricane was coming right at her. He was going in for the death blow, and they both knew it. He picked up more and more speed.

Parker let Aerosmith slip from her fingertips and clunk to the road. Then she pulled the machete from the holster behind her back, and with the last bit of energy she had left, she threw it. The blade swished and whooshed through the air.

The slasher was too big and had built up too much momentum to duck, dive, jump, or get the hell out of the way. There was absolutely nothing he could do, and the machete landed square in his chest.

As if he were a racehorse having a heart attack, his legs failed him, and he crashed to the ground and rolled over and over. Finally, he rolled to a stop at Parker's feet. She knew what she had to do and yanked that machete out of his chest.

Hurricane waved his hands in front of his face as if to say "Stop! Stop! Stop!"

And Parker did. "I'm not going to lie to you," she said. "This is going to hurt."

She slammed down hard and separated Hurricane from his head. And with that, the monster was dead.

SIXTY EIGHT

SHE TOSSED THE MACHETE ASIDE. It had been one hell of a long, miserable bastard of a night, and she felt every last ache and pain of it. Parker dug her fingers into the pocket of her Levi's and pulled out a crushed pack of cigarettes. She hooked one between her teeth and pulled it out. She set it on fire and pulled back on a drag.

Over the years, she had thought about that moment more than she had thought about any other moment in her life. She had played it out in her head a gazillion times. She thought about how she was going to do it and how it would feel. In the imaginary version of this moment that lived in her head, it was always a variation of what was basically the same scene. She would spend weeks or months hunting Hurricane Williams down, and after a few near misses, she would finally catch up with him just as he was about to slaughter another victim. She would say something pithy that would make her sound cool, then they would battle. It wouldn't be an easy fight—she wasn't that naïve—but in the end, she would always be triumphant. The aftermath was her favorite part. You see, after she destroyed the slasher that had destroyed her life, everything from that point on would be perfect. She would give up hunting monsters. She would move to a small town in the middle of nowhere and start over where she could live a quiet life. She would get a job and meet a man. He would be nice and slightly conservative, certainly not a bad boy. They would have children—a boy and a girl—and they would live a life happily ever after. Parker would finally be at peace.

But that was just a fantasy, and she knew it. Parker would never have a white picket fence, and she would never live happily ever after. She was a hunter of monsters, and no matter what, that would never change. She was just going to have to settle for killing as many of those bastards as she could.

THE END

Dear reader,

I hope you had as much fun reading this insanity as I did.

Jack Quaid's sequel to the 1980s horror movie in paperback form, ramps up the carnage and skull-smashing thrills in the next installment in the series. In this one Parker's been out of the hacking and slashing business for over a year. The killer teddy bears, haunted cars and the downright weirdness of it all was just too much for her. But when a couple of kids from an isolated Alaskan town need her help with a slasher that's putting a severe dent in the population, she can't say no.

But does Parker still have what it takes to confront evil head on?

To download Parker's next hack 'n' slash adventure head straight here.

And if you want to leave a quick review for *Escape from Happydale* on Amazon, that would be awesome!

We hope you had fun! Thank you for reading! You rock!

Luke Preston

ALSO BY JACK QUAID

World War Metal Vol: 1

World War Metal Vol: 2

World War Metal Vol: 3

Captain of the Universe

arcade squad

Star Defender

Game Over

Escape from Happydale

Escape from Bastard Town

Escape from Slaughter Beach

Exorcist 90210

The City on the Edge of Tomorrow

A Coin Operated Future

A Fist Full of Credits

For a Few Credits More

The Good, the Bad and the Artificially Advanced

Atomic Pussycat

Hard Boiled: Reloaded

Hard Boiled: Out of Exile

Hard Boiled: Extraction

If you happen to be in possession or know of somebody in possession of any unpublished Jack Quaid novels please contact lukeprestonink@outlook.com

Printed in Great Britain
by Amazon